Waking to My Name

JOHNS HOPKINS: POETRY AND FICTION
John T. Irwin, general editor

Guy Davenport, *DaVinci's Bicycle: Ten Stories*
John Hollander, *"Blue Wine" and Other Poems*
Robert Pack, *Waking to My Name: New and Selected Poems*

Waking to My Name

New and Selected Poems

ROBERT PACK

THE JOHNS HOPKINS UNIVERSITY PRESS
Baltimore & London

This book has been brought to publication with the generous assistance of the G. Harry Pouder Fund.

Many of the poems in this volume appeared in the following publications: *Home from the Cemetery*, Copyright © 1979 by Rutgers University, the State University of New Jersey; *Nothing But Light*, Copyright © 1972 by Rutgers University, the State University of New Jersey; and *Keeping Watch*, Copyright © 1976 by Rutgers University, the State University of New Jersey. Reprinted by permission of Rutgers University Press.

The author wishes to thank the editors of the following magazines and anthologies who published the poems collected here:

Accent, American Landscape, American Literary Anthology, American Scholar, Antaeus, Antioch Review, Arizona Quarterly, Borestone Mountain Poetry Anthology, Botteghe Oscure, Carleton Miscellany, Chelsea Review, Chicago Choice, Chicago Review, Chowder Review, Columbia University Forum, Commentary, Contemporary American Poets, A Controversy of Poets, Countermeasures, Crystal Image, Denver Quarterly, Discovery Magazine, Epoch, Fine Frenzy, A Garland for Christmas, A Geography of Poets, Georgia Review, Guinness Book of Poetry, Harper's Magazine, Impact, Kenyon Review, Listen, London Magazine, Messages, Modern Occasions, New Anthology of American Poetry, New England Review, New Letters, New Orleans Poetry Journal, New Poets of England and America, New Ventures, New World Writing, New Yorker, New Yorker Anthology, New York Quarterly, Paintbrush, Paris Review, Partisan Review, Perspective, Poetry, Poetry Miscellany, Poetry Northwest, Poetry Now, Poetry Past and Present, Prairie Schooner, Quarterly Review, Random House Book of Contemporary Poetry, Saturday Review, Saturday Review Anthology, Sewanee Review, Shenandoah, Southern Review, Stand, Transatlantic Review, Truth, Vanderbilt Poetry Review, Virginia Quarterly, Western Poet, Western Review, Western Wind, Where Is Vietnam?, Yale Review

The Johns Hopkins University Press, Baltimore, Maryland 21218
The Johns Hopkins Press Ltd., London

Library of Congress Catalog Card Number 79-3651
ISBN 0-8018-2357-9 hardcover   ISBN 0-8018-2358-7 paperback

Library of Congress Cataloging in Publication data will be found on the last printed page of this book.

for Patty

While yet we live, scarce one short hour perhaps,
Between us two let there be peace.

—Eve in *Paradise Lost*

Contents

from Nothing but Light   (1972)

Note to the Reader

Many of these poems have been revised repeatedly over the years, always with the purpose of trying to achieve greater clarity and economy while remaining faithful to the informing emotion and idea of their conception. Though every poem has its genesis in a historical moment, its author, I believe, must let the poem find its own way into realization as if it had a life of its own beyond him.

R. P.

Waking to My Name

for Gary Margolis and Larry Raab

> ... for the sake
> Of youthful Poets, who among these hills
> Will be my second self when I am gone.
>
> —*Wordsworth*

After Returning from
Camden Harbor

With the idea of water still in mind,
I say these words out loud and know, therefore,
that I am not asleep; furiously
my mind seizes on green things to assert
its wakefulness: a plain, translucent pitcher,
quiet with milk, on a yellow tablecloth
brightened by morning sun. I observe my lawn,
as if asleep, hazy and steaming with dew
like a white sea sparkling green, according
to the soothing words of my idea of water,
though thunderclouds gathered furiously
over Camden Harbor with sailing boats
rearing like horses against the flat slap
of foaming waves. What stirs my wakefulness
is my idea of you who challenge me
to break free from my tightening mind
that furiously defends itself with words—
on Saturday when water, green as my anger
slobbering like horses, whinnied and surged
from my mind's depths: the nightmare sea where words
are forever wakening, forever asleep.
And though I spoke them, they were not my words;
because my anger toward you at Camden Harbor
snorted and roiled like foaming water,
it seemed as if I stood there still asleep
repeating an idea someone else's green mind
furiously had brought forth. I did not
say what I wanted then to choose to say,
and so I could not feel what furiously
I wanted to feel, according to the idea
that love means choice or that we live asleep—
as beside the water shaking the dock

I failed to will to compose the words
that could free me from the sea-dream of my anger
into a chosen yellow breakfast scene
with a flowered cup and a green pitcher of milk
casting its shadow as you pour for me.
Leaving next dawn, awed from high Camden hill,
the stilled bay water seemed asleep, and we
drove on in sullen silence homeward
through shifting sea-green light of crowded pines
until, as if from nowhere, you explained
that a computer—given six random words
and the idea each sentence must include them,
all repeating in the final line—
composed a poem that furiously made sense.
Still angry, and yet wanting to please you,
a pitcher on a yellow tablecloth in mind,
I asked you what the six words were; you said:
idea   water   asleep   furiously   green   words.

Sorrow

makes itself at home here,
inventing consolations,
opening the future to whatever loves
one needs to fantasize.
Like shade, it adds to everything
it touches
the hue of its own mood;
it is the old oak's signature
on grass—intricate shadows
of leaf and branch.
What would we be without it?
One could dwell forever
in its arrested air
where what might be
breathes its long breath.
No choices need be made
in so personal a world;
even the hooded cowbirds,
stepping through dull April snow,
are images of what one feels.
And yet, when you approach
beneath the oak,
I have no wish for other loves,
ours is enough,
rounded with the sorrow
of our only life
that shadowy contentment
must approve
if love would speak.

A Cord of Wood

By the singed maple tree, the gate unlatches
        expecting another love.
Soon she arrives to wait, counting backwards
        into her darker hopes
as determined grapevines, laden with summer,
        twist toward the sun
up a leaning birch, and potter wasps,
        fattened on dazed spiders
in the cells of their clay urn, emerge to mate,
        to scatter and prepare.
She remembers the entrance to his silence
        where their fixed names
clashed by the kitchen window, and stark clouds,
        in her mother's dress,
strutted their discordant light. Too strong
        not to go on,
too tired to change, she hastens waiting for him
        in the cricket-chime
while an abandoned teapot wails its rising note
        where one wish ago
she left it humming with the dreaming cats.
        He opens his map,
like wood split with a chord crack from an axe,
        to another terrain;
he follows, color by color, remembering
        the law of his doubts
and the cliff sliding down, closing a child's cave
        by the sea where his secrets
swelled out their games, and her imagined hands,
        forever a touch away,
reached for the gate in the cricket-chime as leaves,
        veined like his mother's feet,
shimmered the sun-path with a will that returns
        everything to earth.

In the distance, sharpened with evening chill,
        she hears an axe descend
on the echoing drum of a stump, as a trapped fox
        howls in the hemlock woods
like her father's laugh conceived in his stopped lungs
        the night his failed blood
labored in her heart and thickened her mind.
        And while her husband nears—
county by county, concluding each silence
        with another name,
returning as the sea ramps, wave on wave—
        too hopeful to change,
too strong to deny the map's grain, she feels
        fresh silence quicken
among stones, shuddering each curled tip
        of each loosening leaf
where the gate sways with the wind's flashed will,
        enclosing him
when he arrives. She bears him in her eyes
        unchanged a touch away
as ribbed clouds, poised in wounded light,
        commend him darkly
to his father's charge which binds him still
        to seek her always
by his ingrained image she cannot attain
        which she resists
and gives flesh to in waiting for him
        by the maple tree,
singed in a summer storm, as numbed, late wasps
        prepare and wild grapes
thicken, and piled wood drains according
        to the sun's first law,
until their names, humming with the teapot
        by the kitchen window,
are recorded choiring, soften,
        and become their own.

Rules

It says here: everything
that goes up must come down;
nothing can exceed the speed of light;
mortal things must die;
rules are made to be broken.—
Ah, promises, promises, my dear,
are they to be broken so that no rule
can dominate our lives?

Here, by the shore, the weedy cliff
crumbles a little as goldenrod
pushes up and sways;
I see the late sun's image,
what it was, at light's velocity ago;
a rigid starfish, driftwood
and a crab's claw, form
a minor constellation on wet sand
where I draw a circle
around them with my toe.

Rules are to be broken—
or what is human freedom for?

The waves surge in;
a countering wind flails more foam,
quickens the gull's shudder and glide,
its black eye pure with hunger
before it must descend.

And far at sea, the shark, serene
as usual, rises from its depths,
and then descends, every ravenous
thought and fiber—as they must.

And now I break only one rule,
my dear—that rules must be broken—
so that, hungering, we may descend
to hold a promise
steady as the receding stars.

Looking at a Mountain-Range While Listening to a Mozart Piano Concerto

Looking eastward through my picture window
over the snow, the sun just down, I see
the mountain-range hazing to one shade of blue;
now with the trees obscured, it is a sweep
of shape darkening so flat, one might not
recognize a mountain-range at all —
its silhouette is just a wandering line,
drawn by a hand that might be falling asleep
or else so free that every arc it makes
of rise or fall expresses the contentment
that it feels at heart, although it leads
nowhere but on, and might as well drift off
into another range of further blue.

Brightly the piano asserts its melody;
the orchestra gathers its colors to reply,
true to the law that everything responds,
nothing is left unanswered, that variation
extends the self — as if one's life were made
essential in a piano's theme, departing
then returning one to what one is.
And now again it is the piano's turn,
and now the separate instruments, again
as one, move onward to their chosen end
beyond which nothing else will be desired.

And so my ears pulse back into themselves;
my eyes return to seeing what they see:
the mountain's silhouette — a floating line
leading my sight where visible blue ends.
It is an end in thought — my life goes on,

here I am deciding what to play next
as you appear; suddenly, I recall
when I first saw you, twenty years ago,
playing your flute: I think of waterfalls
in moonlight, orioles in cherry trees.
Your smile extends the silence of your pause,
and then, as if unsure where to go next,
you walk adagio past me out the door,
just as I hear the piano enter in.

The mountain's silhouette is now less sharp.
Something seems missing as the record ends,
spinning with a hiss that empty space
must make between the stars. I move the needle
to the start and light the lamp above my chair.
There are no mountains anymore, only
my reflection in the picture window
like a surgeon's x-ray, ghostly and remote.

I hear the introduction once again;
the piano sings so freshly that I feel
the reason why the orchestra replies.
And you return, carrying the flute
your fingers have not graced for twenty years—
as if a poem had conjured up the past
to ease the fear of darkness and of chance.
The one star in the sky is not enough
to light the mountain-range where darkness holds
the shape my window frame provides. Once more,
for the strings' sake, the piano states its theme;
the violins are moved, they love their part.

Although I cannot see the dark beyond
my mountain's dark, I won't leave love to chance;
I watch you in the window coming near
as if to the conclusion Mozart had in mind.

The Vase

He waits beside the stone wall that he built,
And she comes empty as the vase she knew
Beside her bed, and full as sunburst petals
Glazed roughly on its smooth, empyrean blue.

He won't admit a hidden wall forbids
All touching where invented selves are weak.
He sees she knows what still he can't admit;
And yet they choose green gentleness to speak.

He gazes to the pond: two geese alight.
Within the wall, she softens, leans to him—
A hyacinth between them when they kiss.
He feels her fullness shudder at the brim.

She waits beside the sunburst vase she's cleaned,
And thinks what birds might etch its empty sky.
His hands are scratched and muddy when he comes;
He reaches out to soothe her swelling thigh.

She dusts the vase which drowses in her sight,
And she recalls her need for clenching in;
And she recalls his stiffened hands stretched out
To lift the stone and let the wall begin.

The vase-mouth moans and darkens in the room
And widens as he browses her stark face.
Blue night engulfs them where no meanings stir;
They feel the marrow fear of endless space.

Descending empty to their waiting bed,
They clutch each other in the soil of sleep.
Who are they now as dawn rips them apart?
And yet they choose green gentleness to speak.

Rondo of the Familiar

Beside the waterfall,
by the lichen face of rock,
you pause in pine shade to remember blue
for drawing back, and green
for trust, replenishing yourself
among familiar leaves
with scattered sunlight.
And beyond those trees in time not ours,
you see our children search
for what we gave them, only to find
our love again
in other hands and faces
where our bodies cannot go.
And I step forth
into the scattered light
where you elude me,
though my hands reach out
to share these daily losses,
each beloved breath rounded to a pause,
that still compose our lives.
And the waterfall spills on;
and lichen holds to the rock-face
in the slowness
of its quiet life, deliberate
as the dividing of a cell;
and you remember blue
for each round pause you made
freshening a bed,
washing a window with even strokes.
And I step forth
into quickening light
that restores you and
takes you away, telling my hands
to be true to their green truth —

as our children, preparing
faithfully to depart
beyond those trees,
hold for an instant in the pause
you have composed for them.
And I enter that pause,
though the waterfall spills on,
and pollen dust stains
our windows, and the familiar bed
deepens its repeated sigh,
as you wait for me,
each loss fragrant in your arms,
blue as the early crocus
our children soon will stoop to,
pausing by a waterfall
in familiar time beyond us
in pine shade
by the lichen face of rock.

Departing Words to a Son

We choose to say goodbye against our will
Home will take on stillness when you're gone
Remember us—but don't dwell on the past
Here—wear this watch my father gave to me

Home will take on stillness when you're gone
We'll leave your room as is—at least for now
Here—wear this watch my father gave to me
His face dissolves within the whirling snow

We'll leave your room as is—at least for now
I'll dust the model boats that sail your wall
His face dissolves within the whirling snow
It's hard to picture someone else's life

I'll dust the model boats that sail your wall
Don't lose the watch—the inside is engraved
It's hard to picture someone else's life
Your window's full of icicles again

Don't lose the watch—the inside is engraved
A wedge of geese heads somewhere out of sight
Your window's full of icicles again
Look how the icicles reflect the moon

A wedge of geese heads somewhere out of sight
My father knew the distances we keep
Look how the icicles reflect the moon
The moonlight shimmers wave-like on your wall

My father knew the distances we keep
Your mother sometimes cries out in the night
The moonlight shimmers wave-like on your wall
One June I dove too deep and nearly drowned

Your mother sometimes cries out in the night
She dreams the windy snow has covered her
One June I dove too deep and nearly drowned
She says she's watched me shudder in my sleep

She dreams the windy snow has covered her
She's heard your lost scream stretch across the snow
She says she's watched me shudder in my sleep
We all conceive the loss of what we love

She's heard your lost scream stretch across the snow
My need for her clenched tighter at your birth
We all conceive the loss of what we love
Our love for you has given this house breath

My need for her clenched tighter at your birth
Stillness deepens pulsing in our veins
Our love for you has given this house breath
Some day you'll pass this watch on to your son

Stillness deepens pulsing in our veins
My father's words still speak out from the watch
Some day you'll pass this watch on to your son
Repeating what the goldsmith has etched there

My father's words still speak out from the watch
As moonlit icicles drip on your sill
Repeating what the goldsmith has etched there
We choose to say goodbye against our will

The Kiss

for Kevin

A glaze of ice glistens in the manure
and rutted mud of the plowed-under garden
as the brittle crack and squish of my greased boots
leads me plodding beside my vague reflection
this crisp April morning, as if my image
still were in the thawing earth I planted,
and last year's buried spring still stirred and shined
within the slick clay of the chunky soil.

With boot-grooves packed with mud, my cold cleft toes
imagine they can feel the rising moisture;
stopping by a three-year *red delicious* tree
to scrape a fresh bud with my fingernail,
I see that it is green inside—alive,
having survived the winter in my care.
Yes, it is soft and moist, it has come through
under my care, and I remove the wrapping—
aluminum foil and tape—around its trunk
that saved it from the gnawing mice and voles
who girdle fruit tree barks beneath the snow.
Now on the yellowed grass, the perfect turds
of starving deer, glimmering like planets,
circle the tree, and the faint waft of skunk
brushes me with a puff of wind; I like it,
it quickens my sense at the exquisite edge
where pleasure cloys, where one knows surely
what the human limits are. I kneel
beside another tree as if to dress
a child for school, snipping a dead branch
as sharp sun strikes the creased foil by my knee,
catches my dazzled eyes and makes them tear.
A stranger here might think I truly wept.

Spring blood sings in my veins even as it did
some thirty years ago when I planted
my first apple tree. No lessening
of pleasure dulls the sun's feel on my arms,
a warming chill, or the female curves I see
along the hill that fruit trees make when my eyes
follow slowly, caressing every slope,
then moving on. I am gathering my life in
now with a breath, I know what thoughts I must
hold back to let my careful body thrive
as bone by bone it was designed to do.

A gust of wind comes off the upper slope.
Having followed me, my youngest son,
crying "Watch me, Dad!" runs along the ridge
much faster than I thought he could, launching
his huge, black birthday kite; catching the wind,
the kite leaps for the sky, steadies itself
as the string goes taut. It glides above me, swoops,
floating its shadow on my squinting eyes
that, pruning snippers still in hand, I shield
from shocking light. Designed like a great bat—
hooked wings and pointed ears and long white fangs
grinning like Dracula—it swoops again,
eclipsing the sun, hovers, dives at me;
I see the mock blood oozing at its mouth
and random dribbles brightening its belly
just as it crashes in the apple tree.

I take more shining foil from the tree
and roll it into two enormous teeth,
set them in my mouth like fangs, and chase
my son across the field, running faster
than I thought I could until my ribs
smolder in my chest and my clay hooves ache.
He screams as if the demons of his sleep,
returning from the frozen underground,
were actually upon him—as I catch him,
grapple him down, sink my gleaming teeth
into his pulsing throat and suck, suck deeper
than I have ever sucked, tasting his life
sweeter than any apple I have known.

The Meeting

Her ears and hair are scented by the firs;
Her shadow warps across the moonlit snow.
The story she would tell him is not hers
Although her breath's ghost meets his in their flow.

Still as the ivory face carved on her clasp,
She feels her mother pulsing in her feet.
He sees the house her sorrow cannot grasp
Whose story surges now where two streams meet.

The lichen on the pines absorb the light;
She sucks the moment's silence to her bones.
The wind's rasp on the stream prolongs the night
To swirl her story with the clack of stones.

She strikes the frozen clasp against his cheek;
Her mother's image penetrates his skin.
One window in her house inhales to speak;
Her clenched lungs strain to let the past begin.

Inside the house, like wind, two low moans start.
He grabs the clasp and hurls it in the stream.
Her mother stabs her father in the heart.
An owl flaps from the fir, trailing its scream.

The Thrasher in
the Willow by the Lake

Now I can tell you. Hearing the shrill leaves
Swishing with your hair, I can recall
Just how it happened: the air was thick and still,
Like now, and I could see the lake reflect
The thrasher in the willow tree. I paused,
Knowing that I could never make her change.

I told her that I thought no simple change
Could help—it was too late for help—but still
The thrasher in the willow tree had paused
As if it were an omen to reflect
What the lake desired so that I could recall
Myself in the stirred wind and fish like leaves.

I stared at her among the willow leaves;
If she looked young or old or if some change
Showed rippling in her face, I can't recall.
I know the thrasher saw her when he paused
Over the lake as if he could reflect
Upon his past, stop it and keep it still.

Like this I held her—she would not stay still.
I watched, just like the thrasher, as the leaves
Stirred in the willow tree, and then I paused,
Groping for breath, to see the lake reflect
The blurring wind. Her face refused to change
Enough because she knew I would recall

That moment always, that I would recall
When her eye met the thrasher's eye—and paused,
And might have, but never did, let me change.

Her lake sounds gurgled with the fish-like leaves,
And if you listen, you can hear them still.
Listen, they call in the willow, they reflect

The crying of the lake, and they reflect
The words she might have said to make me change.
Maybe she said them, but I can't recall
Ever hearing them in the willow leaves
When the thrasher blinked and her eye went still.
You know now why I brought you here and paused,

And since I could not change when the sun paused
To reflect the thrasher's eye among the leaves,
The willow will recall your face when the lake goes still.

Advice to Poets Whose Lines Run on in Pursuit of Free Expression but Who Suffer from the Pathetic Fallacy and Who Peter Out, Whose Form Lacks Animation and Whose Spirit Cannot Keep It Up, to Try Using an Iambic Line, Alliteration, Even Writing a Sonnet, in Service to Your Muse

But no one writes iambic verse these days,
You say. Your random meter's limp, so try
To join your beats and let rhyme soothe the ways
Urania can make you soar. For why
Would you erect a loose form that your Muse
Cannot ascend? Submit! True potency
Must serve her needs. Stroke her caesura, bruise
Her Bacchic breast in bold embrace, and see,
She will rejoin by handing you a line—
God's "I Am that I Am," flaming your ears,
Whispering your enjambment is divine
For play, your assonance blasts her to tears.
Coupling in climax, your technique could blow it
Without care where you put your extra foot, you poet!

A Modest Boast at Meridian

No spring can follow past meridian. —*Stevens*

If I embraced a horse, baby,
with all my power,
its neck would stretch like a giraffe's
in one impassioned hour;
and if I nibbled your ear,
an elephant, trumpeting its charge,
would thunder through the forest
of your veins at large.
Take me, my girl,
at the least pleading, I am your own,
prepared to spread largesse among all beasts
who famish at the bone
and wish to freshen at my watering place
where bannered leaves parade the wind's reply:
Be fruitful and go multiply!
Honey, by God, I vow the rains
will swell your lettuce-patch;
the hens will chortle in their huts,
and every golden egg will hatch.
And if, poor mortal girl, the truth
is all that we can bear,
I swear that I'll concoct a yarn
for us to weave our winter bed in
now that lying youth is gone.

The Red Eft

He puts the red eft back beneath its stone,
then dozes on the moss
beside the stream: soon she appears
in hints of light and turns
among the stirring leaves to glow
within each dewdrop
slipping one by one along the ferns.

Beneath the flamed sky
his domed eyelids make, she is a white sun
vaporing the dawn;
he sees her features mirrored everywhere,
her moistened lips
nearing with the woodland quaver
of her streaming hair.

She slides the stone aside—a rose mist rises
spinning into shape
a whirling dust—and offers him
her daughter as his bride
who weeps two crystal tears and easy
as the scented wind
eddies herself in tremors by his side.

She tucks her mother in
beneath the stone, and by crisp light
etches her picture
in the stained bark of an oozing pine;
sticking its needles
to her legs, she does a courting dance
in swirling time.

Now thirty years have gone. Upon the moss
beside the stream, I hold
the red eft in my hand, and she appears
bright as my vanished life.
I lay her form beneath this stone, and find you,
waking by this tree,
and take you mortally to be my wife.

The Twin

He liked to fight. I can remember how
he hit me with a shovel on the beach
when we were four, and I still see the smirk,
when we meet now, that filled his face—as if
nothing has changed, although I know you think
he is a gentle and unselfish man.

He poked my eye with a stick—and that scared him;
we embraced and I forgave him then, and he
promised mother that he'd be more careful.
I tell you this because she knew he lied,
and that encouraged him. Don't let yourself
be fooled, he's more persuasive than I am.

Mother believed him since she had no choice,
he was her son, she had to love him, but she
told me, weeping, that brothers must be true
to their blood bond; she took my hand and I
was flushed and I agreed. She sat right there
on our old sofa just as you do now.

Your hair reflects the gold threads of your shawl—
that rich brocade brings out your elegance;
you have the cheekbones of a baroness.
Despite our failures, to a primal love—
like any mother's for a nursing child—
something in us aspires eternally.

Don't try to change. Your love for ideal love
shines from your forehead almost visibly.
If he could only see it, I would be
at peace and give my blessings as I should.
But he will hurt you just as he hurt me
unless you learn to hold some feelings back.

Give yourself time; don't marry him so soon.
Observe yourself observing him, and see
if underneath his surface ease you can
detect his opposite; it's my duty
as his brother to be the one who warns you—
people end up repeating what they are.

He liked to fight. I can remember how
we embraced, and I forgave him then, and he
told me, weeping, that brothers must be true,
despite our failures, to a primal love;
but he will hurt you just as he hurt me.
People end up repeating what they are.

Survivor

Across the tundra, I saw caribou
Calmly following their crusted routes.
Living as they once lived, not as I do,
My grandma knitted shawls and gave them to
Her daughters; grandpa harvested his oats.
Across the tundra, I saw caribou
Sniffing the wind, uncertain that they knew
That stemmed cloud's knotted bud. Eased in their thoughts,
Living as they once lived, not as I do,
My mother pinched more pepper in the stew;
My father set the corn seeds in their ruts.
Across the tundra, I saw caribou
Break sharply northward as the whole herd flew
In a blur of legs, straining taut heads and throats.
Living as they once lived, not as I do,
Mother stared from her house — the bud cloud bloomed,
Blazing father's wheat as roaring light blasts
Across the tundra. I saw caribou
Living as they once lived, not as I do.

Learning to Forget

Go to, let us go down, and there
confound their language.—*Gen. 11:9*

After three days of rain—starlings
in speckled thousands circling my house—
the Angel of Disaster said to me:
Unwilling to let be, you wanted
to possess what care cannot protect
nor words restore. Now you must learn
even your chimney speaks of your defeat
although your own hands built it stone by stone.
Words were only meant to say *goodbye*.

Your mother's fox stole slung across your crib,
its slick black eyes gleaming at you;
your sister, tumbling from her horse
when the stinging wasp entered its ear—
her eyes turned inward as you held her head;
your wife naked on the moss in moonlight
when the plunging wave of pleasure came, her face
so marble-white that she looked drowned:
those were the images I gave to you.

Turn your ring in your allotted light
and think of circles—not the fox but the sheen
of its blank eyes; picture two windless lakes
seen from a plane—your sister's empty orbs
when her swoon excluded you; recall
the moon reflecting on your wife,
not as a moon but as a perfect shape
orbiting the earth spinning in its place
around the sun. Circles, only circles!

I know how you rehearse your children's grief,
seeking for words that would release them,
freeing you. Do not look up! Your words
cannot make me visible for them.
The last adventure of the will
is to relinquish thought, although your heart
cries still at the cacophony of starlings
circling in their constellation,
your hearth's smoke entering the clouded sky.

Wilt Thou Condemn Me?

Remember me, my son, he paused,
as a man who kept
many ironies in the fire.

Had Hamlet told his father's
purgatorial ghost:
"Rust, rust, perturbéd spirit," that,
he exemplified, would be irony.

Except in death, a son more readily
forgives his father's flaws
than loves his strengths.

The man who needs to meet death
with a final laugh, better
have nerves of irony.

Preferring virtue to reward,
and life to art, he never asked
for whom the Nobel tolled.

The curse of life
is that we know we die;
death's blessing
is oblivion of death.

Consoling her, he soothed:
If I die first, you can support yourself
taking in irony.

Praising her ironic constitution,
he enfranchised her
to read his silences.

When he expressed exactly
what he meant, she knew that once again
he had deceived himself.

The curse of silence
is that we read our own worst thoughts
in someone else's mind.

Fate meant for us to marry,
he assured her; we deserve each other
in this unjust world.

There were no differences
that day to day could not be
ironied out between them.

His whirlwind novel, "Wilt Thou Condemn Me?"
paid their son's tuition, his afflictions
finally finding retribution
in the Job market.

"The rust is silence," artlessly he proclaimed,
steeling himself for dusty death
with a noble will of irony.

Opening his will, she paused and read:
The grace of speech lives when we ask
forgiveness, knowing what
we left unsaid.

The Stained Glass Window

Her weighted chin
cupped in both hands, she leans upon the table
        fixing her gaze now
where the globed swell of a single peach
        in a green bowl
absorbs the late sun's shaft of light piercing
        the bird's blue breast
in the stained glass window; its red wings quiver,
        seeming to lift.
She glares at the perfect curve of shade
        the peach casts in the bowl,
and thinks her husband, pulsing heavily
        in that white room,
is giving birth to his last memory:
        cupped in both hands,
her locked face escapes him out the window,
        down the orchard field
and to another life. Like wind across a lake,
        sudden anger frees
her features from their emptiness, and now
        he knows the cause
of every flight her mind would make beyond
        the field's curved rim
where goldenrod thickened and clumped asters
        congregated swaying
in the morning frost. And on her mouth he sees
        the anger slacken—
he sees her draw the covers to her lips;
        her father, entering
her room, pretends he thinks she is asleep
        and with one finger,
like a boat's prow, moves her hair across her cheek
        behind her ear and whispers

she can hear him in her dream; she listens
          to the ocean sounds
the wind's wail makes stirring in the hemlock trees
          at their field's edge.
Slowly she wakes in the white room; the masked nurse
          passes her the baby
with his ancient, flaming face proclaiming
          the confusion
of his injured sleep. She clutches him and wonders
          what her husband
might be thinking now; she sees him choose the colors
          for the stained glass window
he is making as a present for her homecoming.
          The bird's breast cools blue,
its wings churn red, for it is not a real bird
          that he has in mind
but a geometrical design, overlapping
          rectangles that thrust out
into space where only he perceives
          a bird in flight.
He pauses with the cold glass in his hand
          and sees her leaning
on the table where the sun's blue shaft
          shifts in the bowl
as the peach's light shudders into gray,
          draws inward,
while a final aster glimmers at the field's edge
          in a surge of wind.
And so my mother knew the very moment
          that her husband died,
though maybe I have got it wrong, maybe
          grandmother told that story
to my mother on their farm, although I can't recall
          any stained windows
in that sagging house I visited before
          grandfather died.
And that is why I make this stained glass window
          for our living room,
and why I looked so hard when you sat alone,
          one breath away,
with your glazed face cupped in your hands
          beside a globed peach

in a green bowl, and why I choose heart's red
          for the heated wings
of a geometric bird that you can see in flight
          now at the field's edge,
now in the window, now at the bowl's rim,
          when you return.

Venus

Every delight he ever knew,
he now can see in the night sky:
the red, contented star, borne in his mind,
pulses her light in fullest ease,
praising his conceiving need to name her.
Even his sorrows have taken form,
though not as men: moonlight
mourns beside the still, lake water;
over blue mountains, before dawn,
mist clouds echo on the grass
like longing chords receding
as new melody goes forth.
Spectral music spirals the globe,
widening beyond the galaxy;
he sees himself now atomized
in everything beyond him—sun after
yellow sun. And looking back
where once his universe spun by,
only his thought remains—
melodious and luminous. It is
as if a race of gods, all good,
were sure at last that everything
would find its final shape: red circles,
yellow squares, blue rectangles.

Waking to My Name

Behind me the woods fill with the clashing
      of fresh bird calls—
phoebe, chickadee, robin, wren—
      as the June sun
angles in as if to render visible
      the faint tart scent
of the red pine and the white pine, the cedar,
      the hemlock and the fir;
and behind me as I wake hungry for my own
      flowing, slow arising,
the names keep pouring in—my grandmother,
      Ida, my mother,
Henrietta, my sister, Marian; Patty,
      my wife, Pamela,
my daughter: their faces mingle and separate,
      age and grow young,
as their vowels on my lips, their consonants
      blunt on my teeth,
pluck them back into themselves, into
      the certain image
chosen by my heart again to remind me
      something of each one
has not been left behind, and will not change.
      And behind me the mist
releases edge by edge each rock, and twig by twig
      each shrub, and the mud
glistens as the mud glistened when my grandfather
      woke beside the stream,
and leaf by leaf the mist released the oak
      and its name, and the maple,
and Thomas, his only son, and my father's name, Carl—
      as the birch grove caught
the slant light where the starved fox stood transfixed
      beside a boulder

heaved into its place how many mists ago?
    And my heart fills
with him, and Joseph, his name, quivers in the cold air
    silver with the aspens
as their glazed leaves lift in the hook of the wind
    as he wakes by Ida
and behind him the mist releases eye by eye
    the covey of quails
and the white-arced tail-bar of the grouse
    startled into flight.
And waking by Henrietta, Carl's mind flies off
    after his grandfather
whose name I have lost, and he follows him
    long into the mist
where, for the living sake of love—Patty
    and Erik, Pamela and Kevin, I
must not yet explore, where stones shudder
    in repose, and each tree
breathes its fulfilled life in the forever
    of its single time.
And the June sun dawns upon my hand—
    nails and knuckles,
fingers, veins and thumb—which reaches
    out to the scented woods
and the visible names that merge in the lifting mist
    of my wakening age,
as I fly forth to the radiant green field
    with phoebe and chickadee
clashing, and robin and wren, and my name pulsing,
    repeating with my blood
that most of the full of my life is behind me.

from
Keeping Watch (1976)

Remaining Blue

I am vanishing into my own life.
    The bland, early light
on the blue milk glass belongs anywhere.
    I have lost my grip
on the hatreds that defined me, the old sorrows
    seeking sexual
revelation. Fantastic how the usual
    becomes me, repeating
the change that has ceased to take place, here
    in the same house,
at the same table set with blueberries,
    with the same loves
asking only to be what already they are.
    What can I bring you
that these merging days have not yet brought?
    A new rug woven
with blue flowers like the sage outside?
    A bluebird house
for the garden, the same clay furrows
    on the same slope
of the repeating hill? Blue, I am
    vanishing into blue,
I am son, husband and father still as they were
    the same animal
circling through his day, sleeping back
    into his genesis,
gathering myself again to go on
    in the same blue stride
under the sun. I am no one, I am
    everyone before me,
I go on in my children's lives as they
    vanish into

the same blue air that enfolds me, and keeps me,
        and tells you again
that you can find me only in yourself,
        day by blue day.

Pruning Fruit Trees

Begin by cutting
all branches away
that are now dead.
*It is March. One surely feels
in the air a softness
that has not yet arrived.*
The cut must be made close
to the parent limb,
following the angle
of its growth.
*Used snow inches deep shows
yesterday's boot prints,
my son's and mine, circling
each other, circling each tree.*
Where equal branches
now divide, choose one and cut—
it is not good that they contend
for vital sap.
The cut must be made close
to the parent limb,
soon it will heal.
*The chickadees scold us;
by their feeder they have their rights.*
Don't be afraid to cut—that's it,
cut more, it's good for the tree,
lengthening life,
making its fruit full.
A farmer told me to talk
to the trees. Tell them
"this is good for you."
Speak softly, thank them.
*It is June. Our footprints faintly
circle the trees in the moist grass.*

Like little berries, the fruit is hard.
They will make it, they will hold on.
See, they will hold on, they will ripen,
they will do well.
It is June. I have learned
to ask for nothing more.
I have never
been happier than this.
Tell them they will do well.
As wind flutters their leaves,
praise them.
It is March. The cut
must be made close
to the parent limb.

A Bowl for the Day

I

Under the whir
of your hands,
the split egg slips
into a yellow bowl;
perhaps you think
I am waiting,
as if never before,
to be fed with light.

II

The brook blunders
into itself, replenishes
its passing.
What can I do with my hands
that held back
from touching you
this morning, only
because sun
whitened your hair?

III

Noon steadies and thins
the maple's shadow
on the lawn.
Nothing is on the page
where your hand poises
to write to our son.
I know this,
having wondered myself
what can be told.

IV

We have risen together
for thirteen years.
Our house inhales, reposes.
We are what we will be.
Yet when the woodpecker's
staccato knock
pauses as I pass,
I remember the face
you have outworn.

V

You wax the table, rubbing
in circles
longer than it needs.
The warmed grain speaks:
I belong here;
these rings are my story,
widening,
winding inward.

VI

In the garden
you turn a globe of lettuce
for inspection.
Sunset spreads in the clouds
and everything behind you
advances and dissolves
now as I wait,
a bowl in my hand.

A Spin around the House

I rise from the table, starting to whirl,
    nowhere to go,
cinnamon peach-cake lumped in my cheek,
    my arms streaked out
to my children clutching blown blue glasses
    filled with milk,
moon crescents on each upper lip.
    Stars—I must have stars,
and out I swirl, immediate master of my need,
    my eyes lighting
my body's windy way to a familiar pine
    in its real place
at the first slope of the solid hill.
    Everything spins
in its chosen space—I will it so,
    a star's held silence
pallors my cinnamon lips, and my arms,
    each elbow galaxy,
circle it all in. What shall I do with it?
    I have nowhere to go;
the spectral pine belongs where it is; my children
    whirl with the house
beyond my wrist, moonlit chimney smoke curls—
    a comet's tail.
Nothing is missing, it is all absolutely there,
    I have food enough
in my cheek to last the rushing starlight through
    as pale grass choirs
in its remembered sleep where Ursa the bear
    leapt home, and the Dipper
ladled its milk and pointed tilting north.
    And there the North Star flares

above the pine, above my house, with nothing
    to do but return
circling my arms, whirling in my eyes,
    which now are suns,
and now are gods lifting their blue glasses
    over the spinning table
as their laughter splurges through the galaxy.

The Farm

Briefly at dusk, the birches glimmer,
swelling slowly with hoarded light.
I pause while sliding the curtains closed,
turning inward to our house and night.

As she once was on the woven rug, grandmother
gazes and plays with her toy farm,
arranging the past I enter as I stare
into my daughter's momentary calm.

My father's grandfather's great fire
still inhales and burns in our hearth
where I can see the animals
mounting up the creaking ark.

Across the quickening sea at dawn,
still without wind, the heave of the sun
plucks white cries from the sandpipers.
Somewhere it is already noon

as hazy drizzle on stained eaves
lengthens icicles where a sick child sleeps.
His mother murmurs in my mother's ear
the rocking words the sea-wind keeps.

Somewhere at night, my mother wakes now
in the bed her husband died in years ago.
He has not changed as he prods the fire,
thinking of cows to milk, how his fingers close.

He lowers the ramp, paired animals descend;
the toy farm stirs and shivers in the dawn.
The fire already dwindles in the hearth.
He bends to lace his worn boots on.

The sick child hears him in his sleep
as sandpipers cry like birches in the rain,
and I can feel my father see
the farm lights go and come again.

Nursing at Night

The moon is full, my breasts are full—everyone
    desires them, they are
for everyone. Waking, I save them for his mouth
    that curls like yours
learning to smile your smile. And can you see,
    asleep, that very smile
upon my lips as nursing I lie here
    in the stale light,
my chill toes touching yours, saving your face
    for an empty time?
You think I am yours because he smiles your smile?
    That cleft—he has
my father's chin; and his ears, you will never know
    whom they remind me of; I must
save something for myself as I touch your toes
    and nurse our son
in the stuffed room, emptying my breasts.
    He will leave me,
and you will leave me when you wake,
    smiling your smile,
dreaming of ears that are not shaped like mine.
    Where can I go?
Have you understood the chill of the moon—
    curdled milk
in a cat's bowl, a blood spot
    in the yolk of an egg?
Can you hear me dream? You place your head
    on my free, full breast.
Are you awake? See, I have come back,
    I am here, my breasts
are for you. I pray that he may learn your smile
    for an empty time

in the dusty moon, with my father's cleft,
    waking to strange ears
by someone else's breasts. Full, my milk flows,
    everyone in turn
nurses at my breasts, I save them for you;
    they are mine.

Narcissus

for Pamela

By the east window, narcissus lean in bloom
   as snow romps in the wind.
I am growing again, I have not stopped—
   I can see my falling age
freshly, it is new to me, it takes hold
   collecting my whole mind.
Put on your glasses, my daughter in her snow hat says,
   she wants nothing to change—
for her I will remain myself again,
   neither young nor old,
always there, exact as her need.
   I have stood here before,
happy and sad, watering window narcissus,
   watching the snowfall,
and now it is again the same—yet saying
   it is the same
is new to me, I am older than ever I was,
   although that too
I have said before. I picture the petals
   spread, darken and dry,
the long stems loop over the bowl and down
   before we throw them out.
My daughter does not see that they are gone;
   put on your glasses
my daughter says. The storm thickens and heaves,
   narcissus petals
whiten the air as if with their own light,
   my eyes narrow
in the window and glare, watching my new age,
   collecting what is gone,
the roots—fibers, mottled and yellow,
   we throw them away.

Again I am older than ever I was,
        it does not stop,
downward and downward—it is never the same.
        From their brown bulbs
narcissus rise; my wife says: *the day is clear,*
        it is time to go,
this time I am sure it will be a girl.

Mud Song

Succulent to the bird's hot stare,
                flaring
my hunger's sympathy, the worm stirs
                in the loosening mud,
flutters itself, shakes out great wings,
                exudes
new light, meticulously sings
                itself into an angel,
departing as the rain retreats,
                while in the well
the sky relaxes as my calm repeats.
                As it occurred
I tell you this, you have my word,
                strangely
knowing in this light we live by trust,
                and that we change
each other every morning as we must.

Hymn of Returns

The odor of pine branches, Lady, shimmers your hair,
    and your slow fields
follow lightly in their familiar paths;
    the robin's glance
and the cardinal's furtive skip choir in your noon
    where I keep watch.
My hand is upon you now as you withdraw,
    as beavers ramble
and submerge in their knit pond
    where tense deer sip
and vanish in the brambled blackberry shrubs.
    A crocus glints
in the dawn; the wind bestows your forehead
    with freshened light
as you return the way foamed water smooths
    and solaces the stones.
As snow descends, my hand remembers
    where you were,
the ripe pear in its glow, swelling
    to the tongue and taste.
Midnight moves abroad; I wake in my bed.
    Are you beside me?
There in the pines, your forehead's moonlight
    chills and entices.
You have gone and returned even as I slept!
    Above the mountains,
moist in their dark, where curled deer wait
    alert and hidden
in the blur of leaves, swarmed clouds diminish,
    brighten, and advance.
How can I go on in this single day,
    keeping watch
as you appear and vanish in the pines,
    in the hawk's drift,

in grasses where sheep nuzzle their paths?
        The starred snow flares
to cherry petals and apricot petals,
        lit by your forehead,
whirled by your eyes. I rush from sleep
        into your dawn:
the mist field drifts as I keep watch,
        and my hand remembers
where you are in the scent of the orchard air.

The Cave

The red and brown wax from the candle,
    like stalagmites,
heaves up circling the flame in its cave
    where I see
his Neanderthal face in the fire,
    his watery mouth,
shadows drawing in his cheeks, his forehead
    wanly glistening.
His mate, behind him, hunches by the wall,
    and his furred child
grumbles familiar sounds. He leans forward,
    rocking from the waist,
sniffing, his ears perked through his hair,
    listening for me
as an image shapes in his crouched mind,
    though beyond his cave
where his child huddles his arm, the brunt of wind
    beckons his eyes forth.
He holds where he is as he hears me
    in the rip of wind,
looking long into the fire, and the image
    of my mouth,
blue above ashes, speaks to him
    where the flame
shifts on the wall as I now hold
    what I still have
in the room where my wife embroiders flowers,
    and my children
scramble among their blocks. He turns to the wall,
    and with a stone
scratches animals in procession, a man,
    a woman and a child
behind them, all striding at their ease,

composed, taking in
the good light of their day. Through his eyes
      I see the shimmering
of windy silence; I start another candle
      from the first,
and as we kiss goodnight, our shadows
      merge upon the wall.

Guardians

Wild blackberries are
      glistening their design,
            perfect as snowflakes.
Their juices shudder
      and gather in
            the scent of July
and the moist heat
      as it steadies the air.
            This is the day
our marriage must speak.
      Our children
            stare at us, their spoons
poised at their mouths
      as the moment
            is about to break.
By the window, a hummingbird's
      red throat hovers
            before the pink verbena,
its needle beak prepared
      to stitch the pattern
            of its ancestors.
What can the mown grass say?
      Its scent sweetens the field.
            What can the half-grown pears say?
Each shape is its own,
      like its fellows,
            repeating the sun's light.
This is the judged day,
      so absolutely plain,
            so forgettable —
a single blackberry
      in the dozing field —
            that our vows

draw in their breath,
        cry out in the thorns
                for everything lost
so easily, for each straw
        in the wren's nest.
                The moment is about
to break, though the hummingbird
        holds in the air,
                and blackberries glisten
in the children's spoons.
        We must let it linger,
                we must let go,
our marriage says
        in a cadence of thrust breath
                rising like snowflakes
hefted in the wind.
        Where will the children go?
                Whose hands will know them,
binding them again
        as they choose,
                as we have chosen,
over and over?
        The children's lips
                stain with blackberries—
our moment, married
        to their lives, cannot hold,
                though we held it certain
in our eyes so easily
        a moment's summertime ago
                when the guardian vows
cried out, leaving
        the thorns to stiffen
                in the gusty snow.
This is the day
        our marriage still must speak
                so the hummingbird's red throat
returns to us, even
        as snow quickens
                and each straw rots
in the wren's nest.
        And our children,
                whom we have chosen

beyond us, ripen
    in the blackberry field,
        their relinquished names
binding our vows,
    staining our lips
        in the pungent light.

Maxims in Limbo

1

The happy father
comes to resemble
his children.

2

An early wind hurls roughly
through the willow as if with intent.
The observer sees this
for his pleasure.

3

The only freedom men possess
is to choose
their bondage.

4

On my way home,
the bluejay, high on his perch,
watches me. Are you
waiting for me to arrive?

5

Between the haze descending from the hill,
and the mist at my feet,
I feel my body thicken.

6

Knowledge takes two forms:
noble illusion and ignoble illusion.
The above, for example,
is a noble illusion.

7

The man who attempts to change his wife
dooms himself
to remain the same.

8

Last fall this pear tree
bore a single fruit.
In an odd season, exuberance
refuses to repeat itself.

9

I write these crazy poems
in order to live
a saner life.

10

In a time of despair,
eat bountifully;
in a time of joy,
also eat bountifully.

11

Night wind heaves as
the raccoon lifts his head
from the garbage pail. He thinks
I will not change.

12

Poetry, like revolution,
changes only
the surface of things.

13

It is a noble thing
to give one's life for one's country,
and nobler still
to spare one's country such grief.

14

In the peaceable kingdom,
all but the satirists
lie down together.

15

The happy man
continuously seeks out new ways
to keep things the same.

16

The wild turkey stands in the snow
on one leg.
In the pursuit of comfort even
stupidity is admirable.

17

It is easier to die
for a cause
than to live without one.

18

The happy poet
has no cause,
not even his art.

19

The philosopher knows many things.
The holy man knows one big thing.
The one big thing the poet knows is how
to pretend he knows many things.

20

The happy father asks of his son
only what he can give;
the son knows this
and offers more.

21

The first tenet of the rational man
is that man cannot live
by reason alone.

22

Men breathe the air and
are buried in the earth.
The fish lives and dies
in one element.

23

If we are all guilty,
the idealist is he
who casts the first stone.

24

I would no sooner go naked
among strangers
than converse at a party
without irony.

25

He demanded that reason prevail in the house—
though never will he be the man
his mother was.

26

Writing before breakfast
is like making love to a girl
whose name
has slipped your mind.

27

Ripped stalks and stubble
make colder the cold field.
You observe me, and lo—
I am enhanced.

28

What your enemy knows about you,
your friend
chooses not to see.

29

In the land where the poet rules,
flowers grow only
when watched.

30

The hermit thrush, without looking sideways,
flurries into the bush. The owl
sits in his tree, his head
moving back and forth.

31

The most painful sins to repent for
are those one wishes
one had committed.

32

No matter how one tries, it is hard
not to feel virtuous
when behaving well.

33

The home-fed spider
still spins his web —
but only for sport.

34

The sparrow hawk holds steady in mid-air.
In the flaxen field
the hunched mouse is still.
What must I do next?

35

When discipline fails,
wait for inspiration;
when inspiration fails,
take that as your theme.

36

For a poet, to name
an object carefully,
is to submit to its power.

37

Wind ruffles and erases
the kingfisher's image in the lake.
Yet having said so, I see
it is still there.

38

The trilobite in his stone
has mastered the art
of autobiography.

39

Hell is a place where
there is only bad art;
in heaven (except for hymns?)
there is no art at all.

40

The sudden screech of the wind
is fathomless
because it means
nothing.

41

Obey your wife
when she asks the impossible —
you will improve yourself.

42

When a father's glance
lingers
on his daughter in the sun,
even the sea shudders.

43

In a perfect world, the poet
mourns his useless art;
in an imperfect world,
he mourns his brother.

44

Freely he chooses to say what he must.
His enemy, with envy against his will,
silently admires him.

45

In the best of possible worlds,
only the brave
marry and die.

46

Having performed her obligations
with displeasure, she felt nothing
but virtue.

47

Again wind blusters
through the leaves.
Strange how its sounds
grow familiar!

48

He who despises
comfort,
loves only the future.

49

The same wind blows.
The noblest weakness
is to change one's mind.

50

When a poet chooses a rhyme,
the approach of the storm
holds back.

51

The happy father
rides his son on his back;
they gallop in circles.

52

The happy poet proclaims
the circle, wishing only
for what he has.

53

When your wife
becomes secretive, invent
something to confess.

54

What must I do next?
No image lingers in the windy lake
to tell me
where I have been.

55

In his element, the fish
is almost weightless;
it has no need to dream.

56

In the peaceable kingdom,
the reformer seeks to invent
new virtues.

57

The man whose kingdom
is his belly, requires
a good constitution.

58

To eat or not to eat—
is the moral issue
troubling his digestion.

59

The phoebe on my roof flops her tail.
Perhaps she is happy.
What would she do
if she were sad?

60

I am sad today.
The phoebe on my roof flops her tail.
What would I do
if I were happy?

61

The tender husband
holds to a central truth—
silences help.

62

Let him cultivate
his weakness; without it,
she will never forgive him.

63

Reason extends itself.
Passion is spent by passion.
Renewing himself, the happy man
reasons passionately.

64

I choose you again, freeing myself
from my image in the sun-smoothed lake
and the whim of the wind.

65

The puckered lips of a sunfish
pop the water's surface; circles appear
where my mouth's image was.

66

The poet knows many things. He knows also
many are not true.
If he were a fox,
he would know less.

67

The rabbit zigs across my lawn
thinking I am a fox;
his life depends on it.

68

One eats for pleasure
in the peaceable kingdom;
the satirists stay lean.

69

The fox completes his meal
of fallen phoebe eggs.
That is a hard truth
to enjoy!

70

Wind ramps in the trees
of your dream.
Wake! She has chosen again
not to leave you.

71

When the father feeds his son,
both laugh;
when the son feeds his father,
even the sea shudders.

72

The brontosaurus raises his head
from the brown swamp;
I pause on my way homeward.

73

The wet wind dies and still
cannot find
its image in the lake. ·

74

The willow leaves lift again
in the wind.
I must return when I have changed.

75

Knowing the whole truth, he keeps still;
knowing half the truth, freely
he sets forth.

76

Words are a kind of surface—
like the ruffled lake.
Beneath, the silent fish
feel at home.

77

The spider redesigns its web
in the land where the poet rules.
The change is not perceived
by the caught fly.

78

There are more berries on the bush
than he needs; tonight he will dream
of the wet nose of the fox.

79

The hungry fox sniffs
the wind in the bush; a fly rests
on the nose of the napping man.

80

The autumn lake is white with mist
as geese blurt their red cries.
At your kitchen window,
you do not look up.

81

When a man and woman marry,
the peaceable animals circle
and stretch forth their hands.

82

The happy father lives in a circle;
he knows exuberance is more
than enough.

83

Ask the impossible of your wife;
she deserves no less
for having chosen you.

84

When the sea shudders,
mother and daughter release
their pet gull with a broken wing.

85

The blind man dreams of the windy sea.
The deaf fisherman mends his nets.
The gull cries out from his perch in the cliff.

86

Again, I am heading home.
Two deer stamp the snow before me.
Sleep, old black bear, sleep!

87

Freely the son leaves home.
Someone has planned all this,
neither mother nor father.

88

Through the scorched forest,
the armies advance. One would have thought
nothing could live here.

89

The stone says: I am the cause
of the foam of the stream.
Without me, says the stream, the stone
would never be smooth.

90

I am the cause of the silence that follows,
the thunder says. The silence says
what the poet says that it says.

91

At his slide, the otter's skeleton lies
exposed by the sun.
My children's shadows swing on the lawn;
no wind stirs the willow trees.

92

From its long stem, the shasta daisy
petals shine. I will keep watch
until the next freeze comes.

93

At noon the fish are not eating,
but a boy stands on a stone casting his line.
If I could return now, I would find him.

94

Tanks rumble over cobblestones
among burned-out houses
shredded like stalks. I think it;
I am there.

95

The weak man wakes from his potent dream
still weaker; falling
in his dream, the strong man
wakes in time.

96

Is that again the wind in my dream—
or the tanks
in the wet moss woods the instant before
they can be heard?

97

Heat from my face steams my binoculars.
Against the slanted snow, the puffed owl
thickens himself.

98

By the cool shore, the sun
ignites the underwater weeds
swaying calmly in their flames
until my shadow intervenes.

99

Picture a circle with wind in which hands
separate and touch; even
without faces
these hands are ours.

100

Blue mist purples the distant hills.
Having slept well, I can discern
the grazing shape of the unicorn.

101

When the father dies,
the son becomes mortal.

Feeding the Birds

Incredible perhaps, but for this moment
    all the birds are still;
they are listening. Saint Francis says:
    how blue the light is,
whitening the blossoms of the cherry tree;
    or, it is another
perfect day to save one's soul. Who knows?
    It is not important
what he says to them, what matters
    is his choice
to be their friend, though his companion
    waits impatiently,
thinking of the world's work to be done.
    Francis, by your deathbed
just one disciple saw the angel
    overhead, he was
the silly one, easily distracted,
    looking away
from your stiffened face as the others wept.
    Which friend am I?
Far from Assisi in sloping, white Vermont,
    I feed nuthatch
and chickadee, sparrow and cardinal—
    none remain still,
none listen as I speak. I do not expect
    to see an angel
when I die, or you, dear Francis. Yet,
    incredible perhaps,
I still recite this sermon to myself.
    What folly
to do anything else, in this cold season,
    in this bright place

where I live, blessed because I see
  that it is here!
And the goldfinch, the woodpecker—they need
  the food I give.

Epithalamium

Some say the world will end in fire,
Some say in ice. — *Frost*

What in hell is going on? This autumn flare-up
    startles into song
every red and orange that my eyes
    have romped among.
Never have I seen grass glow so frosted thick,
    the doomed leaves blaze
as if this dawn were the beginning
    of their quick days.
Fornicators arise, this is the dawn
    to dance your heat,
although you feel the final pallor creeping
    upwards in your feet.
Mate eye to orange leaf, mate yellow leaf to field,
    your reds strewn out,
and hotly stroll the hill. This is the promised land
    rejoicers joy about.
Red, red, I come to greet you, friends,
    so come with me
to handle hallelujah voices, flaming
    yellow with this tree.
In my heart's home I know white winter doom;
    I know red bliss.
By heaven, someone must make wedding music
    for all this!

The Map

You follow it to a marked place
where waters turn and light divides—
the story in your father's face
that led you to this cradled child.

Encircled by old hemlock trees,
you lift the child to take him home,
but darkness stiffens in your knees,
and stillness gathers in your bones.

The map's dawn light can only show
the way you had to come, and came—
the lines your father's forehead grew.
You hear the river mouth his name.

Your mother turns and lingers there
to tell you that your father's gone.
Her story spirals in the air
and swirls the map he vanished on.

You study how the light divides,
although you know the place by heart,
but stillness stiffens in your eyes
and will not let the story start.

Only the ending marks the place
that you must go to, and have gone.
The story in your mother's face
encircles you and binds the dawn.

You lay the loosening child down
with waters in his face that say
where you can go, where you have been.
You hear the swirling hemlocks sway.

Where all our river stories merge,
and each dawn's darkness must begin,
I follow you into the surge
that lights my place to enter in.

The Mugger

He will know me when we meet, his blade
clicking open, telling him. I offer
my cape, embroidered in Persia. It is not
what he wants. I show him the secret pocket
in my attaché case and hand him the key.
He rejects it. My Diner's Card, Mobil Oil,
a hundred dollars cash—he throws them
over his shoulder. I show him my mother's picture.
She has always loved me, I tell him
more gruffly than I mean to. He pauses,
lights fire to it, letting it burn back
to his fingertips, glinting on the knife blade.
He says nothing and moves back a step.
A heart is tattooed on his hand. His slick hair
is sweetly perfumed. I take off my tie.
I take off my shoes, my argyle socks.
His lips open, he has one golden tooth.
I stand naked before him. He eyes me
like a doctor. I tell him I was a happy child.
I tell him I am good to my wife,
that my children trust me. He slides my clothes
into the gutter with his foot. Down the street,
where I cannot see, I hear a cry—or a cheer!
I recall the night of my election,
the crowd, and my prepared remarks.
I tell him my plans. I describe my house,
how my fruit trees have grown, how one can smell
the blossoms in the wind at twenty yards—
like his hair. The blade is still. Its glint
reminds me of the pond where I hunted turtles
as a boy at dawn when the mist came up.
I tell him how I made my sister haul the pail
to put them in, her hair golden as his tooth.
He tells me to get dressed, but I have more

to say: change is possible, reason
never rests until it leads men to the truth
where justice dwells. I take more plans
from the attaché case, insisting that he read.
He shuts his knife; I demand that he study them;
they are for him. I have done everything for him.
He tries to move away, but I have him now.
I put the key into his ear and turn it
until he promises to let me keep
his gold tooth as a pledge. He tells me
he has always loved his wife, that his children
are happy. Soon his garden will be ripe.
My plans are coming true. Nothing can stop me now.

October Prayer

Return to the shrunken sun what you know
     you have taken;
remember the sun behind your eyes:
     apples and pears in the field,
the slow vista and the distant lake
     that stunned the hills
with its wavering light. You know
     they are gone
when the sun returns, the trees themselves
     so absolutely there
in early frost that your first eyes
     remember again
as the vista wanders to the lake
     and the lake again
heaves up its light into the hills.
     Once more you know
you have taken in the sun, remembered the thrush
     and its circled eyes;
behold, the thrush is there, an orange berry
     in its brown beak,
as rushed light loosens yellow leaves
     resounding through the hills,
circling the lake, floating like deer.
     And you return
in your yellow voice, pleading *remember*
     the living sun,
it has gone and come back; behold
     it is in the lake
where yellow pears are white and streaked apples
     glow like frost.
Remember the age of the frost,
     it will return
behind your eyes, it is older than ever
     you will become;

it will die, and the sun will die, and you, still here,
            are left remembering
what will come, frost in your eyes,
            the sun in the frost.

Elegy for a Warbler

All her immaculate dolls now weep:
    sing sorrow, sorrow.
Against my girl's window the warbler has broken
    its small life;
let all eyes close, the wind is forsaken,
    nothing can keep.
Nothing I say consoles her, no toys amuse
    or can bring back
her warbler's yellow flight, return it to
    the green hues
of its lost abode: *sorrow, sing sorrow.*
    Where is pale Shelley
and his rising star, where is Hecuba,
    where is stern Milton
watching Lycidas calmly walk the sea?
    My daughter
must not weep alone, let all perturbéd ghosts
    assemble here
beneath her warbler's ruined tree.
    Innocent face,
there is worse awaits you; I am not the one
    to tell you this.
My doll, my warbler, my own grieved life,
    the tears of words
twist in the parent air like the parent knife.

Jeremiah

In that jagged maple tree,
          its torn leaves streaming
                    with October wind,
          furious Jeremiah
shakes his hair, his mouth
          circles to a groan,
                    his eyes see all that strains
          against his will to sleep:
rubble of cities,
          scorched apple orchards,
                    the bloated belly
          of the bone-legged child,
gazing at nothing.
          Why has it come
                    to this? What laws
          have we broken
and break? I cannot find
          the cause in my heart
                    that has brought us down.
          Who has done this?
Is it my brother, keeper
          of cities?
                    Wind in the maple tree,
          old father, Jeremiah,
the way to accuse has weakened
          in me. Your wail spirals
                    in the air and leads me back
          only to myself.
The taste of silver
          sours the breath of the young,
                    and the wise men,
          in the sag of their skins,
hear only the drone
          of the grasshopper.
                    Is it better to go out

by the random bullet
than in this long decay,
        hearing the poisons froth
                in the fields
        and clutter the seas
where fishes' eyes
        film over and expire?
                Have you done this, brother,
        keeper of the fields,
to whom I have given assent,
        believing we are alike,
                that I see your mouth
        in the morning when I wash,
and that at night,
        when I embrace my wife,
                your wife also
        feels my touch?
Are we not one?
        The orphans crouch
                in the cellar;
        by the wall
the sisters weep, having lost
        their inheritance —
                it is forgotten,
        peace is taken away.
Dogs paw at the dung
        in the looted street,
                and the fire takes council,
        sloshing its teeth.
The law! The law!
        We have forsaken its roots!
                The great tree withers
        by the clogged river.
Without the law, again
        we become only what we are;
                cut off from you, brother,
        keeper of the seas,
I seek a cure in my own life.
        Can it be there?
                Who is the enemy,
        with no shadow,
plotting in the room,
        his red pen oozing

at his sweating feet?
Shall I call him my own
who housed in my mother's womb?
Old Jeremiah ghost,
shall I name him brother too?
We go to the stream
and return, confounded,
for the water is sludge;
we go to the field
where the huge-headed calf
drags his tongue;
and the rotting city
plunders the light.
Is it you,
my brother,
who goes there, disguised
in my rejected face,
wearing my shoes?
From my chair,
I see the maple tree
suddenly go still,
returning to itself,
obeying its season,
the law of its kind.
Its red leaves shimmer
in the late, slant rays.
How beautifully it glows,
possessing its time!
Oncoming winter
kindles my house,
making the wooden walls
intimate about me.
I cling to what I have,
keeper of myself.
Cause of the law within me,
just power to accuse
and to atone—sleep now,
Jeremiah, furious wind!
And how would I live, brother,
as our parched roots
shrivel and withdraw,
if I cannot
trust you?

The Hearth

More wood to split
for the evening fire, an ancient purpose
leads my bleak steps
out again into the dusk, cold
with no conclusion.
The axe strokes echo in my arms
like the hollow
of the woodpecker's beech—are they still here,
the perfect arc
and the dead thud ending the descent?
Over the snow
move the muffled conspirators;
they would improve
my life, they would engraft their dream
in my tired arms.
I see them always in the place they have
already left.
How can I resist them? My door is locked.
Why do they need me?
I crouch like a dog and guard the fire inside
as sudden crow calls
pierce the room where my children tumble
their ancient games
in a surge of fingers and frenzied hair.
Startled, they look up.
Something is changing. No good can come of it.
Another log warms the past
in which we live; another crow call
comes and dissolves
as it always has. Nothing has changed;
we are still safe
in our own heat, familiar as night.
But the conspirators

circle my house; they are all there,
      planning my life.
How many are they? My love, are we
      the last ones left?

Beyond My Eyes

Stark branches of the cut-leaf oak claw out;
Beige mist obscures its trunk, baffles my view.
You turn in sleep to watch me watching you.
My eyes swirl white, my swelling hands throb hot.

I turn to watch a doe peer through the mist;
She pauses, legless, sniffs and disappears.
I hear your breathing stiffen in my ear.
I reach for you and feel your sleep resist.

The geese come honking so the mist can speak;
You cry out in your sleep to split the dawn
As if my face were waiting to be born.
The edges of the dry leaves lift and walk.

I shake your wooden arm. A doe appears.
You start from sleep to see stalks clutch the ground
As branches strain their trunks with grinding sounds.
Wedging the mist, the geese flap circling near.

I reach for you although my tongue is numb;
I touch you and tense dawn begins to calm.

The Stone Wall
Circling the Garden

Instantly my fingers know surely
    where the stone will fit.
Its curved weight surges up my arms,
    humming in my blood:
I have waited now a hundred years, knowing
    I belong here.
A twist, a nudge, and there it is
    in its fixed place
in a destined design, balanced in the sun
    which says: *So be it,*
I adore all circles, I commend your work.
    I hear the bees arrive
and the earth revolve, tightening the grip
    of each stone, one
to the other, to the other, to the other,
    in the bronze heat,
ore of my bones, which says: *Breathe in*
    the bees' dark rose
and the dust of the air. And so I do
    as the circle grows
more still, gathering the garden in,
    while bees follow
the odor the wind-lanes waft away
    beyond my sight.
And there another circle tightens, made
    of the shape of stones
as bees revolve and the dust follows
    in the wind-lanes,
each speck shaped like a star, where a circle
    tightens and holds

like a single stone, like the stone
      in the clutch
of my hands which says: *There is nothing further*
      for you to desire.

The Ring

Easing the ring down her finger, he hears noon
    apple branches arc
above them; not one twig obscures their sight
    as they search beyond
each other for an instant, and return.
    With lines etched fine
as in an apple bud, on the gold band,
    a lady receives
her wedding ring in what must be
    reflected light,
for I think the circle above signifies
    the moon. Perhaps
the trees around them arc with the weight of fruit
    that glimmer in the pond
where poised ducks doubly glide in rows,
    or else wind loads
each apple with a weight more than its own.
    Though lord and lady hold
in place, he looks beyond her where the ring
    reveals a couple
entering a house. Over the doorway
    hovers an angel,
haloed, welcoming them in, though perhaps
    only his mother
sees this form if he assumes the couple
    are his parents
as they were. He cannot hear their words
    that warm the room
as owl calls cross the shingles to the clouds.
    Perhaps she asks him
if his mother, when her husband died,
    gave her son this ring
on which his father weds his wife

who stares beyond him
for an instant, fixed in moonlight, and away
        into the apple tree,
beside the pond, her daughter climbs. Perhaps
        he sees her too,
reflected in her mother's eyes,
        as I now see
my daughter whitely in procession
        on her wedding day
with apple branches arced above her hair
        that catches sunlight
like the moon. I hand the groom the ring
        and step back in the house,
an angel guards, beside the moonlit window
        where my mother paused,
when her husband died, and turned the ring half-circle
        where the lord and lady
cannot see. And there, reversed, again
        she waits in apple light,
as slow wind shifts the laden petals
        in her hair, the pond,
under the tree, for him to wed her now,
        as I do thee.

from
Nothing but Light (1972)

Were It Not

for rumors of war and wars
                    men against men
I think I could grow
                    gracefully back to earth
This morning warm
                    for April in Vermont
I sit graceful in the sun
                    nuzzling a pear
sweetening my tongue
                    to my body's roots
Wet it is warm and wet
                    it flows it is good
for the grip of my roots
                    here on this morning
in this sun in this sprouting
                    April returning now
Here I am sower of children
                    there they are
my wife has invented
                    coffee again butter bread
they are good and she is good
                    and my children
have redeemed all sorrow now
                    one bad blood night ago
Now all is grace
                    sun surges in each dew
nothing can spoil this now
                    you are all
every one of you
                    all all are invited
this warm morning
                    to my house

Breakfast Cherries

I am the breakfast poet. I eat everything.
  I have chosen again
to will to hold on, composing my voice.
  This is my last meal,
my children's random quarreling, the same
  last meal that I ate
yesterday. Join me, be with me, gladden
  your tongue with ripe words,
as the whitening sun now shimmers
  the cherries all at once
in their yellow porcelain bowl. They shimmer darkly
  and do not go out
as my children's voices — blue incense taking
  and exchanging shapes —
mingle above the cherries, complaining
  to commence the day.
They are happy, though it is just another morning
  that begins, another
last day and again a final meal to share
  as cherry-pits
harmonize whitening songs in the white sun
  in the porcelain bowl, my poem,
singing what I (what we) will them to sing
  with their children's skulls.
Paradise, in its day, sounded like this,
  darkening cherries
were eaten there, and the pits were thrown away
  with their songs. Nothing
was designed to last, not even the sun, why
  should I quarrel with that?
Now orioles flute in the outside spaces
  unseen, so near,
and falling away. The children listen. I listen
  to their listening

as you approach again only to complain
    that I have wandered off,
bearing your gifts, your cherries, so I return
    to eat, faithful again.
Cherry-pits flow from the porcelain bowl, they cove
    the carpet, they are in my bed;
and now only cherry trees flutter the field,
    drifting into the air,
filling the sun as it blooms red and redder.
    I can eat no more.
It is time for school. The children are quarreling,
    cherry-pits in their kisses,
orioles in their ears. Join me, be with me;
    we have everything to lose.

The Pack Rat

Collector of lost beads, buttons, bird bones,
Catalogue-maker with an eye for glitter,
Litter-lover, entrepreneur of waste—
Bits of snail-shell, chips of jugs, red thread,
Blue thread, tinfoil, teeth; fair-minded thief
(Leaving in my pocket when I slept,
A pine cone and two nuts for the dime you stole);
Reasonable romancer, journeying more
Than half a mile to meet a mate, split-eared
Lover with a bitten tail (your mate mates rough),
You last all courtship long, you stick around
When the brood comes, unlike most other rats;
Payer of prices, busy with no dreams,
But brain enough to get along; moderate
Music maker with moderate powers, thumping
The drum of frightened ground with both hind feet
Or scraping leaves until the dry woods chirp;
Simple screamer, seized by the owl's descent,
One scream and one regret, just one; fellow,
Forebear, survivor, have I lost my way?

Prayer to My Father
While Putting My Son to Bed

for Erik

Father of my voice, old humbled ghost,
   ragged with earned earth,
Teach me to praise those joys your last sleep
   still awakes in me.
What can I hold to? What can I tell this boy
   who at moonrise
Picked a vase of asters, purple and white,
   now holding back from sleep
Another trusting moment, listening
   to my voice,
To what it says? Shall my voice, our voice, say
   beware of the betrayer
In the room of your heart, in this room
   where you brought your asters
Purple and blue and white, those plucked stars?
   I am the one
You have dreamed about who stole your waters,
   devoured your air.
That is only the guilty truth, I must
   not go back to that,
Mourning your death and his death to come
   I have given birth to.
But in your memory, father, ghost
   of my voice,
I choose another theme equally old—
   I speak it simply
As I know how, feeling what I feel
   praising the sun
With you awake in my mind and this boy
   here, here
Hugging goodnight, holding the dark,
   his dark and mine,

With his asters lighting this mourning room
    for you old humbled ghost.
It is good, what I feel is good, I feel
    it has always been good;
I hold to it as you held to it. If only
    my voice, this poem,
This prayer, could hold you back in life,
    and protect my child
When another and another morning comes.

Together We Lay Down

Together we lay down where time begins
Where time has gone a limb sprouts from a pear
Our kisses taught us all the outs and ins
Coming and going always found us there

To hold back is to touch as touchers know
Where time renews a trunk sprouts from a limb
Such growing backwards taught our bodies so
To lose a him in her and her in him

Time gathers to a pause where trunk strikes ground
There is a double speed in going slow
We stopped to find our coming turned around
A pear was what we were where we would go

The seed is in the ground all come to kiss
Where time stops we lie down no end to this

My Daughter

The odor of leaves
    from the drenched (November) lawn
reminds me there is time
    to stop (inside) to pause
watching you (by the window)
    gathering in all I need
to go on.
    Wrapped (for an instant)
in yourself
    you hold your stuffed bird
still as he
    believing he can fly
(that you can fly?).
    Only for an instant
I pause limply
    in your second year
as leaves lie
    in (November) morning mist
their odor thickening
    (perhaps)
pouring in the window
    filling my breath
as I watch your breathing
    as I go on watching.
I am pouring out of myself
    my wounds open
but I am not hurt —
    what cure is this
what shall I do with my hands
    (shall I put them
in the fountain?). The stuffed bird
    twitches the leaves
the leaves fly up into the trees

the fountain (where you sit)
is singing
        angels are there
they pause to drink
        (and the water pleases them).
Daughter what have you done
        I cannot go on watching
my hands are limp
        they would fly from me
to you
        as birds fly (as angels fly?).
Do you see them in your hair
        do you know who I am
who must turn away
        as you rise (with your stuffed bird)
as your second year goes on
        and I go on
though I am healed
        and all others (in November)
who believe me?

The Mountain Ash Tree

It is silent January
        but on the ash tree
                orange berries
      are still hanging.
Who decided this
      there is no purpose in it
              though I can imagine
      each to be a globe of blood
a soldier's epitaph or
      a sparrow's or your own.
              What is the point—
      that we live to die
and die to be remembered
      for some purpose
              in a globe of blood?
      I have no purpose
though here I am
      remembering you
              remembering
      the ash tree
while it is there
      outside and down a hill.
              The winter sun is still
      a great light
in the heavens.
      It says to me behold
              the orange berries
      which I recall to do.
It says see
      they are not alive
              though they are here
      to console
or to bring back sorrow
      as you so choose.

                    I try
              I say to myself
        as the sun speaks
                    (beasts and men
                              and worlds
              have died in its sight)
        that soldier there
              is not your son
                        you are not
              the sparrow's wife.
        But sorrow returns
              there is no
                        escaping sorrow
              of other men
        almost your own
              sorrow of small birds
                        and beasts of the field.
              I shall remake the world.
        I shall cleanse the waters.
              The sun says
                    let it be so.
              I shall make pure the air.
        That too is good
              says the sun.
                        Cities shall be gardens
              and only natural death
        shall live.
              I approve that
                        best of all
              the sun says
        and the ash shall flourish
              and the sparrow breed
                        and the soldier
              shall lie down whole
        in his own bed.
              But that does not
                        console
              it cannot be.
        I must
              without purpose
                        find something
              to hold to

                                                    108

as I hold
        to you
                and you to me
       while we go down.
I open the door on sunlight.
       I walk in the field
              through the snow
       down to the ash tree.
I put a berry
       in my mouth
             bite it
       it is hard and bitter
and without purpose
       and I stand there
             your image in my mind
       saying to the sun
we are still alive.

Everything Is Possible

I am becoming a god!
At last!
I knew I could make it.
You always told me so.
I knew I could never rest
Until I did it.
Now in my left hand, see
My first made meadow.
Let there be a fox
With a magnificent, rufous tail
Echoing windward behind it.
Does that please you?
And behind that stone
I have shaped, see
The vixen's den lit
With the polished eyes of her cubs.
Do you like that?
And there in my right hand
Pulses a lake;
You can hear the roots
Of willow trees sucking
Toward the source of its flow.
What color fish
Shall I put in it?
Shall I make them symmetrical?
Shall I fleck them
With random dots
and inscrutable blotches?
Everything is possible!
You always told me so.
Let there be a child!
May I plant him inside you
And let him grow

To tend the fox and tend the fish,
Humming the meadow,
Whistling the shape of the lake?
Could we rest then?

The Hummingbird

hums with her wings, I am
   in flight again. Surely
I can master the air suspended
   at a rose to stay
while the sun pivots around me
   another hour, another day.
I have entered her heart within
   a fraction of an inch,
within her nest no larger
   than a walnut shell, laced
with lichen and with spider webs,
   while wind bulges
the leaves, and the petaled sun
   pivots around me. My wings,
you cannot see them, I am here to stay
   as the rose lifts up
forever in the sun. I pivot
   to my nest, warming
unbelievably tiny eggs,
   for that is the way,
it must be repeated at another hour
   on another day.
Having entered her heart,
   I whirl with the sun,
in flight unbelievably with wings—
   a hummingbird
who sings the ruby color at her throat
   sipping the rose
as I hum sipping at the sun.
   Leaving her heart,
her nest, her eggs, I am in flight
   until the petals
unbelievably burn away
   in the humming air
at another hour on another day.

The Moment After

You are gone. In a circle of trees
        I am left
with your absence in a space
        I had to imagine.
The pine needles glare, one by one
        they are emerging
from the mist — or are being
        engulfed. Preceded
by his cry, a crow appears,
        vanishes, his cry
trailing after him, his shadow
        in my eyes
which see that you are gone except
        for your faint hands
which the mist has not yet taken away,
        nor given back.
I have loved you — I will love you forever
        as long as I can.

At This Distance

it is difficult to tell
whether you are approaching
　　or moving away.
Noon sunlight on the snow,
　　the still field nothing
but light, holds you
　　where you are,
a dark form that keeps my eyes
　　from closing.
Suddenly I know
　　you are returning
with great news, something
　　that will change
our lives—a flower,
　　never found before,
having pierced the snow,
　　whose delicate odor
restores a past
　　in which we start again.
As if from underground,
　　wind lunges and blurs,
the whole field
　　seems to lift up,
tilting away from me.
　　You struggle,
holding the flower
　　from the wind, pushing
but moving backward.
　　Throw it away!
Do not breathe it! I cry
　　to you, unheard.
The wind twists gouging
　　into its hole,

the field tilts back,
   nothing but light.
If it is not too late,
   if you return,
I will offer you
   a single bloom, one
with no power, smelling only
   of plucked light.

The Children

          The children are burning
     I must stop it
I must stop it at once
         though they are not
     my own
not yet my own
         yet I do care
     I must choose to care
they are all innocent.
         We must go backwards
     we must return
to a simpler time
         was there ever
     such a time
and if not
         if such time never was
     a time without care
can I still believe
         that it might have been
     and if so
set out to find it?
         But the children are burning
     their faces like wrinkled fruit
their eyes sizzle
         their lips burst
     now even as I speak
as I compose myself
         to find the facts
     and judge and in judging
kill
         and in killing
     stop the killing
bringing back

that carefree time
that never was
though I believe it
if only
for the children's sakes.
Fool fool
I cannot kill
my way backwards
to fruitful innocence
what temptation
have I eaten
what careless dream
have I composed
that I might kill
in righteousness
in innocence
to save the world
the garden
dead almost to its roots
with all its holy devils
for were they too
not children once
and have they not
children they care for
of their own
who will be burned
burning with my own
as we all burn down
in the carefree flames
with the odor of fruit
with nothing to save us
nothing
but remorse
composed at last
as we stop to look back
at what we cared for.

Apocalypse in Black and White

When all the rubble of our fears was piled
Smoke upon dust, white silence upon smoke,
And one black horse reined loose by one white child
Broke by as black the bleating white waves broke,
Amid the first, the last, the dying dead,
All burning voices burned into my head.

One silenced cry, one charred black mouth, was all,
Its voices cinders searing my white eyes.
We wailed together at the wailing wall,
Blood from our hands and hearts smoking the skies,
And all the dead with all that dying spent
Cried out this death was more than death had meant.

Into the rubbled wall, the smoke, the waves,
Rode one black child spurred free on his white horse,
The white-charred men burned down in their black graves
Fear of white death had finished its black course;
One hope, one fate, one death, one brotherhood
Was all I saw, and all I understood.

The Ruler

Having wandered through the tumult city,
    having asked why men,
Afraid of death, are not afraid to kill,
    having pondered it
And cast my vote, I arrive again
    renewing myself
At the bed where I buried my first tooth.
    Behold! I remove the pillow,
It is still there, obdurate and gleaming,
    reflecting old wishes,
Old defeats. I must confront them. I must
    discipline myself.
I must return to the source of things,
    to the source of eating
And the course and end of appetite
    if I am to rule.
And so I do—I replace my new tooth
    with the old,
Fitting it carefully, molding the gum
    around it, tapping,
Stanching the blood. The tooth begins to throb
    with memory:
My mother with an ice pack on my cheek,
    my father glowering
Disapproval at my screams. Behold!
    I have caught them
Each in an eternal pose, I have set
    all of us free!
We know now what we are and can
    transform ourselves.
Discipline! I have done it with discipline!
    I shall rule you all,
Having mastered myself, having traced the past
    to its hurt roots

And controlled my screams. I shall finish
    my book explaining
Everything. I shall be elected. The votes
    are streaming in,
The people clamoring for me. They need me.
    I bring them freedom
In a tooth. Behold! In my cupped hands
    there are two teeth,
And four, and now a skull, and now
    a skeleton
Kicking his feet, throwing out his arms,
    screaming *Control yourselves!*

He Dies Alive

Thinking of brightness, my friend sucks
    the lemon light,
taking its taste to his roots,
    which the rain remembers.
And my cause is to speak
    without weapons
in my voice, without blame,
    to tell that his eyes
still love the lemon light and
    the orange light
and the inward glow of the plum
    whose juices flow
where the rain remembers, though
    the receding stars
speed outward to forsake his love.
    And I praise the brightness,
though it will be lost to the eyes
    of my friend
when his tongue withers in his head,
    for my cause cannot
rescue his eyes, which soon again
    will return to stones.
And my friend sucks his last taste
    of lemon light
as my cause speaks, without blame, of stones,
    of natural causes,
hoping only to cure in myself
    the star's wish
to forsake the life in my friend's last glance
    at the lemon light.
Let the brightness now forever burn
    in our cause,
my friend, with us touching, living
    our separate deaths!

The Screech Owl

With an embryo's face, a wail, the screech owl,
    shredding the night,
opens the tale I live in, having chosen
    to remember now
the humped stone I escaped from
    many shapes ago.
And the mouse returns to his young from the oracle
    where vexed wind taught him
only his own speech and the hunger grip
    with which he arrived
as dust answered with a mouth of dust, with entrails
    where the oak roots groan.
Soon enough we will all meet, the owl inspired
    from his hollow tree,
eyes facing forward, and the mouse blinking,
    repeating to his pulse
the fanged warnings that he learned at birth.
    It is my tale—
it is all inside me—here where a ripped kiss
    begins the world
in my belly where the sea blurts forth and oak roots
    grapple a stone,
its lips straining toward its thought of the sun.
    Here the prophetic eyes
of the mouse drain backward into my hooked hands
    as the owl retreats alive
with his kill to his young in the hollow tree
    where a stone throbs
at its roots, trying to escape what it must know,
    what I cannot choose
not to remember though all kisses bleed,
    that its tale

will lead it where I am—in the mouse's eyes,
    in the stretched belly
of the owl, to begin again, to choose
    again to continue,
until the screeching sun sucks back the sea.

Terminal

The voices come to depart. Within
        the terminal,
they gather rigid as wooden benches
        in crowds under clocks
whose memory has gone out, making
        private sounds
of vanishing. They have all come
        to leave,
each one has come; though I cannot
        find you among them,
all are disguised in something about you.
        How shall I call you?
Why have you let this voice wear your shoes,
        that one your shawl?
Are you here in the glance of a child pausing
        by the sea,
hoping I will know where to find you?
        Wearing my father's beard,
the wind arrives with its wet, salt lips,
        telling me to forget,
but I cannot forget, and I call to you
        in the only voice I know,
the one that repeats and goes on,
        as the voices turn away,
softly leaving step by step,
        taking you with them.

The Plea of the Wound

If only I could remember if
   I got this way
In self-defense. And you, if still alive,
   do you mistrust me yet?
Have you forgotten me, speaking as I do?
   Smelling my fate,
The question it asks, the insects choir on.
   Their time has not passed.
My bleeding starts again, it has never stopped,
   has yours stopped?
It is happening. Yes, it is all happening.
   I have said it before
But have never believed it. I shall say it now
   but will not believe it.
And the stunned dinosaurs burrow deeper
   into their tombs,
They have stopped bleeding forever except
   in my blood or yours
If you are still alive defending
   your right to go on.
As the insects feed, I hear your voice singing
   of the pity of it,
Asking forgiveness, asking what have you done
   to me, speaking
In my voice that has tried and is trying
   to remember
The cause that will make it all happen,
   and is happening,
And indeed has already happened even now
   as the insects choir
And the dinosaur oblivion deepens
   into the spaces

Where my bleeding goes, unable to remember
   how I got this way,
How I started off with you in this way,
   how this way,
Though I plead against it, leads me on.

Her Black Hair

blows within his dream as lifting snow,
within the snow's descent, begins again.
Upon his window-ledge, he sees two crows.
Laughing asleep, he starts to touch her when
snow swirls beside the pillow where she lies.
He strains to stroke and wake her with his eyes.

Thrashed snowlight fills their mirror and explodes;
his outstretched body tumbles toward the sun,
traversed by silent, slowly flapping crows.
He strains from sleep to call her once again,
but sees her start. She knows he cannot stop.
The mirror meets them rising as they drop.

Two crows perch on a rigid hemlock limb,
wind glistening their wings as their bills meet.
He dreams he touches her, she touches him;
he hears her in the laughter of his sleep.
The window in the mirror starts to flow
and lifts their rising with the lift of snow.

And now his laughter startles her awake,
and hemlock branches now begin to rise.
Behind the windy mirror two crows break
into the light exploding from his eyes.
Awake to his own starting, she is there—
sun on her arms. He touches her black hair.

Now Full of Silences

Now full of silences, now full of sighs
    as light wind lifts
Over stones shining like little moons,
    the lumbering animals come,
Filling the last spaces, to enact our fate
    They come in pairs
As they have always done, freely
    without choice,
Without delay, without the words
    for necessary doom
Which tell our tale, and their tale,
    and the story
Of the gods who once watered here
    sharing their sighs
At the taking off of immortality.
    Never abandoning
The past, here we are as stars shudder
    in a different element
Keeping watch over the stony fields
    we are learning to forego
As the animals leave for the last spaces
    full of silences
Which our words fill emptying themselves,
    watering the final pity
We once taught the gods when we walked
    among them.
I cry out for the animals to hear—
    that I am with them,
That never in my heart have I left them
    or abandoned our tale
And its past that rivals the fertile stars.
    But the animals,
Their blazing bodies dazzling the wind
    I will always remember,

Do not understand, and I cannot explain
    as I tell this tale
With the animal history of love in my eyes.
    I lead them now
Into the story which I cannot choose
    to abandon,
Seeking the sighs gods use to speak
    farewell
That will bind us forever in silent spaces
    of holy remorse
Where wind settles and the stones stare
    from their pallid light,
And hand in hand, as we have always done,
    we walk into the past.

from
Home from the Cemetery (1969)

The Stone

If I could move. If my dark speck
       could become an eye,
My rough edge an ear. If I could smell
       that dark shape hushed there—
If it is there. If I could stretch to touch
       that stirring shade—
If it does stir, if it is there.
          How can I change?
How can the flecked dark of my eye see
       that dark flecking
Somewhere out there? Can my ear's rough edge
       hear the swell of a shape
Outward, making the space stir
       so it fills between us
With something to hold—as a claw can hold?
       Can I grow a claw?
Can I grow a foot to move that claw?
       Would it take too long,
Longer than a claw can remain a stone?
       Are there stones
That can stay still? Are there stones
       with no specks for eyes,
No edges for ears? Have they flecked backwards—
       dwindling to what?
Would it hurt to grow a claw? Would a hurt claw
       hurt what it held? If the dark
Thing frightened me, I would eat it with a mouth
       and two claws that could grip.
The dark swallowed inside me, would I
       tighten to a stone?
And if I frightened the dark thing,
       would it eat me?

If I cried DON'T EAT ME, would it hear?
       What would it do?
How would I make that cry? How long can a stone
       remain a stone? Can a stone cry?
Can a claw? Can a mouth? I will try.
       I will try to find you
If you are out there. If you are out there,
       try to find me.

Still Life

Mold flutters on the bread the milk shades blue
Blue window rain dries now to gray to white
White in your eye takes on a hollow hue
The blurring word whirls pulsing into sight

Blink hard the tablecloth returns to green
White apples in the bowl return to red
Your face is forming on the knife's white gleam
Warm shadow mold now burgeons into bread

The bread is cut my body's mold goes dry
My body bleeds blue apples in a bowl
White rain weeps down the window of your eye
The knife's white gleam blurs fading in a hole

Green apple love weeping blue air white knife
You kiss you kill you tender me my life

Self-Portrait Looking out the Window

The eyes are posing again. Pluck out their whispers!
Blur the left one that likes corners, will not
Look back, staring through the grackle-dark:
ARE YOU OUT THERE? What can the nose smell
In that thick paint, but itself strung downward
Into throat, into lungs? Can the one ear in sight,
Touched blue, be listening? I remember the other,
Snooping behind your words to find you.
The red circles I have put near the lips
Are lights stuffed to remain wet, and the splatter
Of whites slashed outward are, in their way,
Looking for you. Harder than breathing,
A vacuum is sucking in the cheeks.
Cave shadows squeeze the dregs of bears
Sleeping the winter through. Beneath
The table—where elbows thicken and apples
Glisten inward and a water pitcher sweats—
Where one cannot see, does the left hand grasp
A bird that I can free to find you?

The Last Will and Testament
of Art Evergreen

Jack fell down and broke his crown
And Jill came tumbling after.

I

Hearing the bell in his skull, a scattering
     of birds,
The angelus dying dingdong,
     I imagine
Art Evergreen, eaten, beaten by age,
Wishing to prepare himself to meet his Maker.
     And since I too,
Old enough to know I will grow older,
Hear my body's dingdong dying in the blood pulse
     of my river ear,
See my hair itched loose beneath trees in puddles,
My cheek pocked in the moon, my eye glinting
     in a carving knife;
Having passed myself in the mannequined glass
     of store windows,
And watched my shadow's hand in doorways
     grasp at me
Or vanish, broken up, among stones clacking
     on a brackish beach
Where a bronze boy rides his white horse in the foam;
I, Jack Jackson, choose to write Art Evergreen's
     last testament and will,
If just to answer back the voices,
     echoing from sleep,
Of ancient reptiles munching bones,
     though maybe
Something to be trusted will yet spring up
And save Art Evergreen, who, somewhere in my heart,
     is dying.

II

And so I, Art Evergreen, still seeking
      in a lover's ear
Snug passage to a cave beside a sea,
      hereupon, dear beneficiaries,
Affix my family seal—Aardvark and Zebra.
To my first wife, Jill, I leave my record collection,
      A-M remaindered by divorce,
My hi-fi woofer, my tweeter, now obsolete,
      paid for on time.
Dancing midnight maneuvers pizzicato
      on her parents' couch
Brought the trombones of contention
      to a cymbal clash.
Ah, goddess of paradox, how sweetly sorrow
Deepens love!—I have no regrets
      for having regrets,
So, Jill, travail to the winds,
      there is more melody
For me, for you, although no airs may blow
      so freshly blue
As those elaborate slow liberties, with strings
      attached by wedlock.
And to our son (who hasn't written in years),
May he count himself blessed: our follies
      shall excuse his own.

III

In a bar, he orders drinks in French
      for his orang-utan,
Who loves him, brushes the hair from his forehead,
      a tear from his eye;
Or they are arm-wrestling on an apple-dappled
      tablecloth while
Begrudging dinghy sailors and a coxswain stare,
And the lonely, enchanted-again, junior-year-abroaders,
      still chaste at bottom,
Cheer their favorite on, and will offer him
      succulent figs—
Depending, of course, on who wins. Or perhaps
      while the captain quivers

Down the spiny, swordfish, deep-sea lanes,
My son, in his wine-dark attic,
          learning Greek nouns,
Anchors with a girl who harbors a grudge,
Prepares to abandon him on a whim.
          More health to you, son,
Her hoarded womb will repent this day,
But you will be digging graves for pottery bits
          and the bones of cities.

          IV

Under the oleander, fragrant and poisonous,
          the lovers lie,
Pumping the earth in its orbit. My son—
Following his nose on his errant own way
          to the Grand Union
For a salted ham—stares with abashed
          astonishment.
Relax, it is your grandfather, my boy,
          I recognize his rump,
Enjoying the first of his last flings
          with a shepherdess,
A flute in her hand. Look, she winks at you
          over his shoulder,
And points with her flute to a thatched cottage
With a picket fence up the chicory road.
          Wait for her there;
She cannot take your grandfather lightly,
          but it is you she loves.

          V

Ah, I enjoyed your enjoyment of that, Art!
          A man should take pride
In the rise of his son, though venomous juices
Bulge a woman's veins. She lullabies
          what she is born to lose,
And babbles in a dream the dread her baby
          will get gobbled up
By the wolf sucking his tail at the door,
Or the hyena sniggering at the window.
          And then she hears

Her infant son's voice thicken, fuzz bristles
About his little groin, his nails stiffen
        and must be clipped.
Can she turn to me when her garden wilts and peels,
The lettuce leaves slacken, buggy strawberries
        sag oozy and brown,
And no longer can her fingers flex the shepherd's pipe
        or set the centaurs skipping
Through the dandelions? I danced to it once, Jill,
        sun-blind, drunk on air,
Before we thought to ask why our son fears us.

        VI

I leave my eyes to you, Jill, both nearsighted.
Wonder back through them to sunlight whipping
        white on tacking sailboats;
Or sledding over the dip of a hill,
See the unfurling smoke of children's voices.
        Past rainbow conch shells,
See salt-shiny toes of sandpiper girls
        swinging hands;
Yellow trefoil fields; masquerading skunks;
        the clown-glee of raccoons
Parading through their moony paradise
        of garbage pails;
Ripe dogwood berries, blood redder than the sun's
        own embryo;
Latticed fern shade flicking like witches
        whirring among cedars;
Gray pine bark mildewed green to the north;
        and in a somber room,
Remember where a woman's napping arms
(Yours, my dear) curl like purring, umber cats.
        O eyes, I shall miss you!

        VII

No, Art, the advantage of being dead
        is that one sees nothing.
The drowning captain stops his thumping
        in the boarded room,
His son's red dump-truck fossils in his eyes.

Walking the crab-strewn beach at night, I smell
    the clay cliffs loom;
The shucking sound of the receding sea
    loosens my legs; my owl eyes
Orbit from my head, floating like stars,
    and I watch my boneless body
Spiraling away, moon craters
    where my ears were,
And I know I will never enter them again
To hear sand slushing at my feet.

VIII

I leave my ears, cleaned, the hair snipped off,
    to Jill, my second wife.
I admire a woman who likes tidying a drawer,
    can wrestle with spiders,
Knows how to charm a sinkful of vegetables.
And I forgive her not forgiving me
    my infidelities
Which, I regret, she took personally.
Perhaps, Jill, you'll need these ears someday;
    teach them new tricks!
They know the whistle of the wary hermit thrush,
    the chickadee's flirting chatter,
The white-throated sparrow's lugubrious melody
    (fine word, lugubrious),
And the lugubrious horns of tugs at night
    on the neon river,
And the formal romancing rumble of frogs,
    lugubrious too.
All these things they have learned by heart.
    O ears, I shall miss you!

IX

Ears resemble a channeled bay swirling
    with gongs of buoy guides.
But only being deaf and blind
Will soothe the captain dry-docked in his mind.
    Ah, but a woman's ear—
Like a petite garden, the lobe like a pear,
And drawing a stream eastward on her back

makes her shiver;
And the squishes, the liquid oboe sounds!
        But that's all over with—
I mean if really I were Art Evergreen.
Try screaming, Art, like an escaped lunatic;
        or a soldier
With his leg shredding off, his friend
        afraid to touch it;
Or a wrinkle-necked man by a fogged window,
His riding boots locked in his closet,
        writing a will;
Nothing held back, the black hole of his mouth
        stretches wider and wider,
And the tongue twists out absolutely wordless.

        X

Please place my tombstone, staunch trustees,
        (gift, tax deductible),
Behind the dorm in the nook of the hill
        among the apple trees,
Where mushed fruit mashes with the knock
        of rollicking hickory nuts,
And shivering kids in the goat-ribbed nights
        shrivel their butts.

And cut the stone to my last rhyme:
        Art Evergreen lies trusted here
Who loved professing in his time
        about the pterodactyl slime,
Though, phoenix-like, his meter rose above,
        in conference with a doe-eyed dear,
                professing love.

        XI

There are flowers in my room. Did you think
        I was *nowhere* writing this?
Yes, here I am, humming an old air, real
        as that yellow vase
With the crazed serpent's tongue chipped at the rim,
        and the wild asters
About to wilt. Not true, one cannot *see* them

about to wilt,
But they will be long dead by the time I am
              Art Evergreen, or you.
The morning valley mist grazes like my son's
              blue hippopotamus,
And through the screen window, dotted with hairy moths,
The bare wind wafts the scent of cut alfalfa,
              and I again enjoy
Our evening stroll around the rolling pasture:
Cow flop, blazing heaps of gold
              in the orange light,
The thick sweet odor broadening my nostrils,
And the silhouette of a horse under an arm
              of a dying elm,
And buff-breasted swallows arcing out
              and back to the barn shade.
At any moment, Jill, we'll hear the wail
              of an early owl.

              XII

Where is Jill now, I wonder, how does she look
              grown grandmother-old,
Flab swinging from her arms, lumpy veins
On her thighs, her hair tinted blue, her eyes
              weepy with sunlight?
Do her breasts flop in the tub? Does she think of rivers
              when she squats to pee?
Do water snakes still frighten her?
Have her fingers lost their quickness? Her toenails,
              are they barnacle green?
Does she powder her shoes and fold her panties
              quaintly on their shelves?
Do orioles lighten her long afternoons,
Or arpeggios of rain on the pebble roof?
              Does she remember
The labia throb and the nightly soothing
              sleepward rocking?
I'll bet she'd laugh if I snuck up behind
And goosed that withered, wrinkled, sunken rump.
              That's birdsong for you!

XIII

Or maybe she is dying this very minute;
Maybe she swerved off the road to avoid
      a squirrel,
And on her snapped-back head nose blood
      flows over her furry lip
Into her mouth, and her stark eyes stare.
Perhaps she sees, at the end of a cave,
      a thatched cottage
Glowing outward in waves, its door open,
The white-haired gardener putting down his shears,
      beckoning, smiling,
As roadside laurel blooms up and up,
      and the cave mouth closes.
Or she lies shrunk in her wedding negligee,
      pushing as in childbirth,
While cancer munches her like a weasel,
      stripping a chicken bone,
And the acid saliva curdles her tongue,
And nothing moves in her mind but her own pain—
      not even a cry for help.
Or maybe out of habit not yet dead,
She thinks her mother is dying or perhaps
      giving birth to her.

XIV

Art's fears turn against Jill, against me.
Who among you will frigate him home
      to the Bronx Zoo
Where each plump captured creature safely
      stalks its prey?
There elephant lies down with tiger,
      tiger with Art's guinea pig,
And the zookeeper's beard floats blithely
On the winnowy wind, while honey eyes
      hosanna his garden plot.
If caged by a vow your windward mind drifts off,
Smooth your fingers over the bow of Art's lips,
      yes, like that,
Lie back and sniff the dusty August grass

Where clover bees fumble and suck,
      and whisper lisping
Your sister got better grades than you at school,
And your father squeezed the budding girl you were
      until, frightened, you cried.
If Art lies with you, he does not mean to deceive,
      but to keep you near him.

XV

My nose I leave to my able, older brother,
      who raised Cain as a kid,
And broke up with his wife because
      she didn't bathe enough,
Refused to buy a deodorant, claimed
      it gave her a rash.
I slept with her while trying to patch things up
      between them, liked her,
Though I was more conscious of perspiring,
      I confess, than usual.
And nuzzling her, I would recall
As many odors as my mind allowed:
      Bacon smoke, midnight coffee,
Urine (after eating asparagus),
Baking garlic bread, rice popping in curry,
      honeysuckle, a stable
With sweaty leather and warm straw,
Apple pulp rotting, dripping wisteria,
      weeds slushing in a cove,
A cedar chest with clammy plaid blankets
      and beetle shells,
The sour stairway to a tenement room
Where, in neat rows, she grew geraniums.
      O nose, I shall miss you!

XVI

So, brother Jack, though you filched a fortune
      from a Broker's Trust Dad owned,
I leave twelve dollars worth of pennies
      to your son (when I was ten
I stole them from your piggy bank);
And to your wife, I leave an autumn elegy

of horny gourds
And falling fog where rabbits nibble wreaths
In a sog of leaves as bluejays raid
      the graveyard bittersweet.
Sound the triangle, blast the horn!
One high-proof toast, one final double play,
      before we gallop on
To territories westward! To your true son (or mine),
      dear Jack, I also leave
My six-shooter, my baseball mitt, my corkscrew,
      and my trusty mask.

XVII

Time for lunch! I could eat a palomino!
      One stops for lunch, kemo sabay,
Even when writing a will; maybe the pain
      merely was hunger.
The whiskered captain, spitting an apple seed,
      brings me chicken soup.
Of course! I am taking the prescribed ocean voyage,
      my legs wrapped,
My buckle loosened, my phoenix-feathered golf cap
      jauntily awry
As dolphin stitch together sea and sky
      on the harbor's horizon.
Two muscular boys play badminton;
One misses because he noticed me.
      Perhaps he knows I am ill.
Why won't he rest his hand on my arm?
      What is he afraid of?

XVIII

Damn you, Art, get on with your will!
That bronze-browed boy is not your son,
      though he resembles me
And will not forget the shadows drying maúve
      around your eyes
Or the lizard shoes sticking stiff from the blanket.
He will not screw the desperate girl
      after the captain's ball
Or confide in his brother's fiancée.

He reads into the night,
    Plays solitaire, dreams of melony ladies
        ripening bugless,
And writes letters to his mother
        about the crumbling
Of old cities, and markets scenting the dawn
        where persimmon luster
Streams nimbus glory. And the fish are so fresh
        they quiver and gasp!

XIX

To my third wife, fearful of heights—
        Jill was her name—
I leave four eloping daughters whom
She feathered an embrace ago
        with teasing frills.
So fleetingly a woman's body fills,
        then empties, empties.
She primed those daughters nesting in my hair
        for giddy flight,
And stubble fire would prickle my skin
        down to my toes
When—echoing through a cobbled street
        bleary at night,
Past fountain satyrs dribbling in their beards—
        I heard wings beat.

XX

And when Jill sees a drunk or a beggar
        or a scrounging alley cat,
Does she still get teary? Does she still pity
The berserk strangler for his compulsions?
        She could have nursed a werewolf,
Closed her eyes and stroked his matted fur.
        She bought four doves
And thought they sang like clarinets;
To me they burped like coffee pots.
        We argued, and I got
Each one an olive branch, opened the window
        and sent them on their way.
But I wildly wept when, gingham-plumed

One August afternoon, my four birds flew
        (Jill moved to town),
And I meant those tears, good though they felt
        pell-melling down.

XXI

This lugubrious document is evasive
        because men kill.
Control yourself! Now let's shake hands. Art,
A fishbone in the stain of his smile,
        has something for you all,
Though without his eyes, his ears, his curious nose
        which, you recall,
He has given away, how does he know who is here?
        Are any of you waiting—
Lovely but unloved, with merely a flaw
(Say a wart on your cheek), curls twinkling you neck,
        your bottom balanced,
Your calves smooth, and knees set starward
To pirate on the sunset cinnamon seas
        and sing your sorrow well,
Meaning *you* who hear the ding of the dong
        of the angelus bell?

XXII

You are fidgeting; the world is going to pot,
        and I have not improved it—
For which my illegitimate sons, all twelve
        (at last count), thrice deny me.
What knocks will unbetray their hearts,
        and fly them, as the cock crows,
Petering out home where they belong? No,
        I must not hope for that!
Let the wind mutter in the marsh grass,
The geese scatter, the ears of the doe perk thick,
        and the sheathed hunter
Stiffen to his cramped thrill—I shall let be!
        Blind Jill must choose
To reject my eyes, and Jack cannot accept
        even my nose,
And I must lead it snuffing with me

Where, stuffed with dust, it will be mine
        forever and forever.

XXIII

And my grandfather who put his false teeth
        in a glass pitcher of tea
When he went to bed and they would grin at me
In the morning when I went to wake him,
        what is left of his bones?
And my uncle Jack whose teeth popped out
        when he sneezed under water
And they bit four plump ladies before the summer ended
But could not be found by me or even the lifeguard,
        what is left of his bones?
And my other uncle Jack who used a wooden leg
After the war and could dance the jig—
        so one night late
I stole it and chipped off two of the toes
But he always let me beat him at slapjack
        because I cried if I lost,
What is left of his bones? And I wonder if anyone
        saved his wooden leg.

XXIV

Rummaging photos, her eyes bewitched,
        her lips puckered by age,
Mother confused one person with another—
As when father hiked me to the bass-swelled pond;
        I was just four, tripping
On the clutchy roots of trees where brown bears
        scratched their shoulder blades,
And bird-shadows whizzed through hissing leaves.
        Beside the path
The forest fluttered with bunchberries—
White, four-petaled flowers, hunched in a dance,
        and I said, "Daddy,
This is the first time in my whole life
        I've explored real woods."
But mother was wrong, that's what father said
        to his father,
For grandmother used to tell that story.

I leave thanks to my mother for retelling that tale,
    the calm of her hand
Still on my head when my fever passed.

XXV

To my fourth wife, Jill, I leave the baby bib
    mother left me,
Because Jill loved to eat, and though stalk-thin
    when we married,
She blossomed swilling olives. It had nothing to do
    with calories,
The pleasure of savoring olive tang,
Sucking in the coy tongues of pimientos,
    happied her fat.
Olives, after a while, should cloy,
    but not for Jill.
They quickened her eye, bloomed fuzzy peaches
    on her belly, plums on her elbows;
They dimpled her knees like ponds plinking
    with polished frogs,
And made her fertile as turtles sunning
    on their logs.
Now don't forget, the fact that I chose her
    accrues to my credit;
Most men have a taste only for tragic love.

XXVI

And my father said to me on my fifth birthday,
"Son, if you could live your life again,
    what would you change?"
"Well, Dad, I'd change my turtle's name from Jack,
    but I'm happy here."
That's all mother remembered, and the story
    seems complete,
Though one long laugh gagged shortly
    in my father's chest:
Pulse gripping pulse, she called him in the cave
    where dropped tides trapped his rowboat
On the hidden rocks; she watched him shrink
    into a cowboy hat,
His fist jerked back into a gun; she saw his lips

149

Move to a scare of frozen bedroom eyes—become
         a choking fetus lung,
Not even saying "forgive me" or "goodbye."

XXVII

My son, this second, must be flying to see me
Or composing another draft of a letter, trying
         to say what he feels.
He is afraid, perhaps, that I mistrust him,
That I suspect he wonders what I will leave him.
         Or maybe he is rich now;
Or discovering a cure for heart disease;
         or his pregnant wife,
Scooping the seeds from a cantaloupe,
Watches the sun flare in a toy dump truck
         stranded on the seashell rug,
Humming, thinking of nothing, or maybe of me.
         I remember the downpour
When he rode me bareback through the mountain path,
His thighs gripping my neck, his hands in my hair;
         lightning lunged through red clouds,
And he said, "Do it again, Daddy!" I have only
         a war bond left to leave him.

XXVIII

Nursing the contrived bone of your memory,
         stroking yourself
Beneath the sheet, your eyes like scarabs
         set in the pillow,
Trying to will something to her, to me,
The gorged words gurgle in your throat.
         Don't betray us, Art,
Pretending your bed is the *Mayflower*,
That you are hoisting anchor to find new lands!
         Don't speak in parables
About a valley where the corn unsickens
On brittle stalks and a blind girl sees
         the sunlight thicken
In the apple trees. Can't you spare us
         some of your pain?
What will you leave to my orang-utan

Wearing orange blossoms on his brow?
        Don't let us down!
A man's death is what he makes of it!
        Where is your divine scorn?

XXIX

And to you, God, unwinding the wound
        of your labyrinthine navel,
Your horse's mane, coiffured in desert stone,
Hooked over your hyena ears, and the judgment
        crocodile teeth,
And the burden lines of your behemoth cheeks
        (probably a hippo),
And the portending forehead of leviathan
        (probably a sperm whale),
And the buoyant, suckling, female breasts,
        nursing wolves and lambs,
And the staff, the rod, the lightning bolts
        cocked in your hand,
And the tickling fig leaf (added later),
        and the cloven, dancing feet
Caked with home mud by a familiar tree,
        and the wings,
The tire-fanning wings with feathers overlaid
        hue upon brightening hue
Into a rainbow spanning the covenant, seascape,
        breath-filled void;
To you I leave the wishbone of a nightingale,
        and my olympic shuttlecock.

XXX

That's better. Accept your Maker's will.
Rod in hand, unmasked, leap up naked hi ho
        out of bed, prancing erect
On your pet hog, your cape streaming, singing
        The Star-Spangled Banner;
Embrace the bassoon-playing nurse, named Jill,
Swearing you will be faithful forever,
        you have found her at last.
Yes, I believe you, and I'll open your will,
The rising angelus bells of my blood

        clamoring your praise
Dingdong, dingdong, as the window crimsons,
        flushed from the bay's light,
And the gulls squawk in the cliff's clay shade,
While beneath the colonnade vaulting
        the stage of the air,
Your daughters, your sons, your brothers, your wives,
        millions upon millions,
Gather chanting for your final words.
        They shall have them.
How long can I go on writing this,
        keeping you alive?

The Weasel

Since the king's death, nothing removes my fear,
Though I have all his power now. I remind myself
I am now king, and it is true. Here

In my hole, lord of the milk and garter
Snakes, I stand on guard. In the bleached meadow,
Hawks dip down like sunlight searing water,

But I know them, and though they circle,
Glutted with white space, though they have snatched friends off
With a look blank as his death, I wish them well.

And beyond, where grass in the wind is quick
As my own tongue, over the rabbit's smoking belly, flies,
Hovering like notes, make usual music.

I had long ago accepted it—the song that quivered
Happiness through my teeth. But since his death,
It has gone sour; I taste it from my liver,

Licking the puffed wound where my heart lies.
I breathe the spoiled milk scent of the air,
And know, the first time again, I too must die.

Since his death, voices call that have no name.
After the catbird's cry, after the squirrel's
Chitter tweaks in my nose its damp dreams

And the bullfrog's rumble fattens his belly
For round sleep, I cannot tell her
As she dreams, clutched to her spent day, beside me.

Did she twitch like that in sleep before?
I cannot remember. And though it seems
That even now I love her more,

An ease is gone, our nest is rearranged.
The walls of the hole are packed down tighter;
The entrance to the hole is changed.

The fear grows in me like a child. At odd
Hours, it tells me what I should not do.
If this goes on, I will believe in God.

Hunger

Never again, the wrinkled forsythia cried,
No, not once more, not ever again at all,
They wept, *you have never loved us enough.*
My father slammed the refrigerator door
And did not return. Newspapers flapped,
Circling the room, perching on the window ledge.

That week my hunger began. At first only
Snacks and nibblings: a piece of lampshade,
Electric wire, knobs from the radio.
At night I fasted. Then, at my birthday dinner,
I ate the Wedgewood dishes, the maple table,
The Danish chairs. I ate, I left nothing
In the room, the house, but walls, windows,
My children and my wife. The forsythia cried,
Never again, and I fasted. Robins,
With berries in their mouths, perched
On the window ledge. The refrigerator filled,
New chairs appeared, a table, a tablecloth,
A flowered rug, pictures on the walls.
Radios burgeoned my ears, cameras my eyes,
Tools sprouted from my fingers, wheels from my legs;
I used them, ate them, picked my musical teeth.

In my steel stomach, in my wired groin,
I felt the kingdom of my power: I felt
My bones stretch arching to a vault.
I devoured more nails, more bolts, more hooks,
Windows, walls and roof. Possessions such as these
Required more children and more wives.

All this, of course, is just a dream, for there
My father fasts forever in his bed.

The forsythia cry *never* in the long rain,
They cry *you have never loved us enough;*
And my children, what waking can I feed them?

Don't Sit under the Apple Tree with Anyone Else but Me

Created for whose sake? The praying
Mantis eats its mate. Hatched,
Two hundred or more eggs scramble away
Eating each other. Among the outer leaves
Of plants; along flower stems;
Sometime on branches; sometime on walls;
Seen by some, yes, looking in windows,
They wait for lady beetles, they wait
For honeybees. Do not judge them.
They are, I am, what we are.
They can be kept (in separate cages)
As pets, and will take pieces of apple
(See Genesis, chapters 1-4)
From your fingers, or sip water
From a spoon. With imagination
(Familiarity?) there is little
One cannot enjoy in heaven or earth.
After they know you well, they cock
Their chiseled heads at your approach,
Asking, as I do, to be loved?

Love

It's not that I usually try for much
The first time with a girl, and though
She was attractive, nice breasts especially,
Full but with a good lilt to them,
Still it wasn't as if I was smitten
Or really out of control. So when I eased my hand
On that fine left breast and she seemed
To like it and slipped me a look that might mean
Uncertainty or confusion or you-belong-to-me-now,
I figured what-the-hell and started unbuttoning her.
But when my hand wiggled inside, I found
A rabbit. "Keep it," she said, quite openly I thought,
Nor teary or wistful as if to indicate
That's-far-enough. So I coolly fingered back (was she
Putting me on?), but it was a book I found this time—
One, as a matter of fact, that I hadn't read.
"Thank you," I said, and I wasn't merely
Being polite; after all, what *can* you say
To a girl? Another try: This time I found
A necktie. At first I guessed she might be
Criticizing my taste, but no—it was my style
And quite expensive. My birthday's not till June;
Consider, what could I feel but gratitude?
And is man ever able to hold himself back
When a good thing comes his way? I was getting
Excited, and in I plunged again: a potted plant,
A wallet, a pair of gloves, theater tickets, binoculars,
Another tie, another rabbit, more books, and then—
A breast! My god, did I do something wrong?
Is she getting tired of me?

Stillness

I have my love stopped dying you this day
This day this dying hour the dying stops
The skeleton I feed still dies away
White bleeding rises and dark bleeding drops

The ripest berry tightens back to green
This bleeding hour the bleeding stops this day
This is the stillness that I meant to mean
The skeleton I feed still comes to stay

The bleeding light I speak drops from your eyes
And overflows the stillness that I mean
White evening wettens stops dark morning dries
The tightest berry ripens back from green

My skeleton rise up by blood we live
You stop the stillness that I die to give

Professor Zinn Watches
a Storm by the Sea

Whinnying through his spittle, like the sea,
The white horse hoofs against
The lightning-struck cloud split pig-blood red.

He does not understand electricity,
And is, therefore, irrational.

He races foaming to the far fence, trying
To shake loose the rider who is not there.
The sweat in his ears pricks him.

He has never been beyond that fence. He kicks it
And recoils. Tricked gentleness puffs up his eyes.

If I could only explain about electricity.
Poor beast, he has no one to hate.

He pauses, cloaked within a great oak tree.
Opening like the mouths of bass on sand, his nostrils
Burn with forced patience.

That is a mistake—he should not stand beneath the tree.
It conducts electricity, especially when wet.

In the slobber of wind: leaves, branches,
Are the hair, the arms, of a woman who has lost control.
"Go!" she screams, "I will never forgive you!"

There is no need for such behavior.

Lightning has lopped the tree. *I told you so.*
Breaking past the fence, he runs, as if roped, over the field
Through the gnarled underbrush at the cliff's edge.

Kicking toward heaven, over and over he rolls down,
His belly bare as a stone in the next lightning flash.

He rises on the beach, stares an instant, whinnies at the sea,
Then goes galloping without direction.

"Come back, dumb beast, come back!"

In the electric light, I see his left hoof
Splatter a washed-up squid
Like the thick-haired head of a doll.

Ballad for Baby Ruth
(or, *How to Burst Joy's Grape*)

Chocolate kisses! Milky Way! Forever Yours!
   And Baby Ruth at home
Amid the not-so-alien candy corn:
   white tipping the top,
Then orange tapering fat to yellow,
   and yellow yellowing;
While out there in the Milky Way—
   another fruit-flavored,
Life-savoring sunset: orange of apricot,
   orange of kumquat,
Canteloupe orange, orange of nectarine,
   and apple red
Blinking blue to plum, and banana yellow
   pulsing up from green.

   And here is a honey-do gumdrop kiss
Forever yours until our teeth decay,
   And here is my vanilla bean,
     And here is my milky way!

Shaped like pears, frolicking yellow
   flute notes leap;
Bassoon-round-sounding plums bulge purple
   to the edge;
Are you filling up, my Baby Ruth?
   Has your quick
Lip-licking pink tongue tasted yet
   the whole, hoped message
Of orange light now mellowing yellow home:
   marshmallows fondled gold
By fire-flame-flutter; tang lemon in chill
   hot-summer tea;

Peach marmalade; or blueberry jelly
    with peanut butter?

        And here is a honey-do gumdrop kiss
Forever yours until our teeth decay,
        And here is my vanilla bean,
            And here is my milky way!

For the candy light comes up, surrounds,
        yellow spreads out,
Purple thrusts in, flavored with malt, with salt,
        with egg whites whipped,
And your teeth shiver, your gums quake,
        your taste buds rise,
Nourished with vegetable oil, with syruped corn,
        with butterscotch, with milk,
And your left ear blushes to a horn's red flare,
        your right to an oboe's blue.
And the orange light comes up, Baby Ruth, comes out,
        goes in, for you, for me,
Where last the first void was, and is,
        and will forever be.

        And here is a honey-do gumdrop kiss
Forever yours until our teeth decay,
        And here is my vanilla bean,
            And here is my milky way!

Burning the Laboratory

Nine months I have been planning it.
The time has come, nothing having changed.
Almost like clockwork, the watchman, shortly
After midnight, begins to doze, his head bobbing
On his shoulders like a dazed swimmer's.
Occasionally a twitch will wake him, hair
Skittering in his eyes—but I must chance that.
About one-thirty, Dr. Wunsch, always last,
Will leave, followed by his hunched back
And unfinished thoughts. He ignores the watchman
Who, in his sleep, expects him. I will
Smack the watchman's head with a pipe
(Hopefully not injuring him),
Take his keys and, guided by the floor plan
(Sent to me by the State as a public service),
I will, in less than four minutes, achieve
The basement where I will set three time bombs
I myself have made: one by the heating plant;
One by the electrical control unit;
And one just for good luck. I will leave
By the delivery entrance in the back.
If all goes well, the building should not
Collapse, but fires should break out all over,
Though, of course, I cannot know how
The various chemicals and equipment
Will react. Perhaps, on the second floor,
Fixed brains of white rats will jerk open,
Prescribed memories and the tinkered past
Will fall away; perhaps a saving word
Will shape the split lips of the leader rat.
It is always possible—like peace.

The Unificationizer

First, you must reorganize yourself.
Later, the rest. It is not enough
To redistribute parts. How can you simplify—
      say an elephant—
Merely by replacing tail with trunk (since surely
Thinking and eating from one end is crude);
Too many memories still remain.
No, you must start with cells, basic units.
Attachment fibers must be cleansed, they are gummy
      and they ooze.
Though specialized work, articles are available
To the layman—IF, and this is important,
      he has the incentive.
You need not, for example, tolerate anger.
Anger units can be cut out, but preserve them
      by quick freezing:
Someday, who knows, a use for them may be found.
Take pains not to damage adjacent cells.
      I warn you,
They are easily destroyed and sometimes seem
To destroy themselves without being touched.
      You have made progress
If, next morning, when you lay your egg,
It is perfectly round. That is exciting.
You will have found new strength to work late hours,
Not to rely on the company of friends,
To break the obsession for touching girls—
      in sum, to commit yourself.
After removing the hate cell, invisible poisons
Must be drained out. A vacuum pump, with a tube
Attached to the ear, is cheap and efficient.
      Test yourself then,
See if there is not more powder in your skin,

More white in your fingernails, and note
You are less distracted by peripheral images,
The dead branch of a tree, a dog waiting
For a stoplight, the stain in the gloves
        you gave your mother.
The egg, now smaller, is no longer to be eaten,
And less hurt is required to produce it.
        Next, vestigial organs
Must be excised; there are more than you think.
The balance you get from toes, for example,
        causes a loss of caution.
You do not need toes if stable and self-contained.
There is a cord that begins in the neck
        and goes down to the rectum
Which, after two neat snips, can be pulled out,
Easy as reeling in a fish. This operation
Should be done alone with mirrors.
Notice then that the egg has become still smaller,
        the shell more mushroomy,
And before you must pack cotton in your nose
        (bits of wool socks will do)
You will detect, emanating from the egg,
The odor of families rotting, stuffed
In a perambulator, pushed by a bearded nurse
        without a nose.
That is no time to turn back. Let me repeat.
        That is no time to turn back.

The Ghosts

The roused ghosts shimmer through the door alive
They shed their sheets they smooth them on our bed
They kiss night's mildew from each other's eyes
Their tongues are words of all they left unsaid

Their breathing quickens breathlessly awake
All in this hour alive we breathe their breath
I know them by the moaning that they make
I know them by their dying of our death

A human mouth glints pulsing in the sky
Passing our window shadow on the snow
An arc of eyes these little moons swirl by
The ghosts clutch all lost quickness that they know

Our flaring fades they vanish into sheets
As at the door our quick son beats and beats

Lying in Bed

I Childhood Illness

My face in the pillow, I hear
The splitting of icicles.
My window brightens
From reflected snow light;
A woodpecker cracks at my pane, knocking
The snow fluff with his tassled head.
"No need to get well," says the bony bird,
"She will care for you in your bed."

II The Lovers Falling Asleep

A white flower opens,
Born in a blue-cracked vase;
Petals shudder, flick apart,
Drifting to dust on the tabletop
Where a lame moth nicks its path;
Whisker-twitching rafter mice
Nibble seeds. Beetles
Purr against the screen;
A green fly grazes and whirrs;
Tossed by a drift of shade,
Thistles preen
In the thick rain-pause; a drop
Slips over a thorn.
I stretch back from sleep
As your mouth opens
But does not speak.

III His Wife Nursing at Dawn

In the cedar by the window, cooling
To green from flaring white,

Baby robins wheedle their necks
For worms. The mother redbreast stops,
Feeds the flick of their tongues.
First light speckles your arm,
Shifting like shallow water
Sliding whitely over its shade.

My son, will he receive my death
Watching his wife on a white morning,
A morning white as this one?

Home from the Cemetery

I

Pennies glitter where his eyes should be.
I stand, trembling wet, before him.
Rising from his back, he plucks the pennies away
And reads to me from a leather book:
"From almost invisible eggs, the embryo whale
Grows humped out huger than a dinosaur.
The mother, swaying like an ark, nurses her young,
Flowing great streams of milk. Their ancestors
Moved from the land, for water buoyed
Their bulk above their element."

II

Rubbing pauses of ocean silence, whales
Rumble like boulders jostling beneath the sea.
Hissing, then slushing on the sand
Like a collapsed lung sucking air,
His body clenches in, shrinks to a hunched animal.
"I cannot hear what you say, father!"
The smile of his teeth is bone;
A dry wind groans from his stomach;
He scurries into a hole's grip. "Come away,"
Mother said, her face blank as moonlight.

III

Your face stares featureless, parched
In the slatted stream of dusty light,
As you gather yourself to our bed's edge.
I start, hold back, and cannot touch you.
You stray to the window, blink up the blind,
And rest there lost in your silhouette,
Twisting the initialed ring father left me.

Bacon curls in the pan, smoke rising.
Sitting, you water the window violets,
Then sip from a cup circled by painted swans,
Tinkling the rim with your teeth.
A milk crescent blossoms your upper lip.
Brushing a hair from your robe, you rise
To arrange the spice jars on the shelf,
Naming them beneath your breath:
Rosemary, coriander, ginger, marjoram.

IV

A black car double-parks, motor whining.
In a store window, a mannequin,
Dressed in velvet red, holds her arms out.
A policeman with white gloves looks at his watch
As children wait. Slumped in doorway shade,
The building half-burned from the top, a beggar
Squats like an owl. His face is puffed bread
Gone sour at the dripping mouth.
He looks at me, sees nothing, asks nothing.
Cars poke over the street, squawking
Like pigs pushing at a trough.
Above the ripped lot, circled by doors
As if it were a makeshift ark, derricks
Clank through the sky then streak down, fishing
Like prehistoric birds, preying on mud.

V

Blue flesh blurred beneath his eyes.
In the bathroom before we left, mother
Gave him pills, white powder on her cheeks.
As he leans, starting the next oar stroke,
Nose-pocks come at me. A beaver
Whacks the water with his tail,
Plunging under. Strung through the gills,
Two trout drag by the boat, flipping fins,
Twitching, trying to right themselves.
The kingfisher preens high on a spruce,
Jabbing his wing feathers. Father says nothing.

VI

What were you thinking, father,
When thick blood clogged your brain?
Could you hide the shame of your failed strength,
Crouched in the slack shade of regret?
Emperor of melody, where were you
When she hummed, soothing me to sleep
On the bough of the knotted dark?

VII

Through the bridge's girders and wires,
Like filaments when the eyes are tired,
I see coves where sailboats graze,
Nibbling the breeze-plucked water grass
By the rickety docks where kids
Fish in the bottom slime for eels and shoes
Hooked where the soles wore out.
At the edge of sight, over sun-stained water,
A school of whales passes, spouting, going
Because their bodies go, sailing the seasons
Without knowledge of their beloved dead,
Nudged by an odd wind to our tame sands,
Prodded by sticks of Sunday bathers.
No, I see no whales out there, water
Is whipping the glint of smoothed-down rocks,
Barnacled for the curled feet of perched birds
With fish curved in their mouths.
SEAVIEW CEMETERY 10 MILES

VIII

Nestled in the sand like a turtle's egg,
His salt-scrubbed skull—rejected by the sea,
Jellyfish in its sockets—opens it hinged jaws
As the flung tide swings in, saying:
"Hammer two nails in the log an inch apart.
Hold the chicken, son, so its wings don't flap.
Put its neck between the nails,
Then when I bring the axe down here,
You let go, stand back and wait.
Once I saw a headless chicken lay an egg."

IX

Painted like a doll, rose-apple cheeks,
Pink lips, polished nose, he looked
Tucked asleep. The casket door slushed closed
Like the quick suck of water down a drain.
And down, lowered down, held by purple ribbons,
He sank down in the weed-fringed grave hole.

X

Repeating through the dusk pine depths,
The white-crowned sparrow's whistle glides.
An otter slides one last spree down the bank.
Over the hushed lake hovers the kingfisher
In the late flare of spectral light.
Plumed with caught fire, his crested head
Cocks back, eyes open, strikes like a spear,
And the gouged wound of the water, emptied
Of one minnow-sparkle, heals over.

XI

Sitting on a sled, squinting blank
Into the snow-shine, up the hill
Mother pulled me in her fur cap,
Her voice thick as oatmeal,
Her nose red as a strawberry.
"Time to go home and eat," she said.
Trout browned in popping bacon fat.

XII

Pale, her look anonymous with grief,
Mother clutched me at the grave, eyes
Searching the empty answer of deep space.
Her face still beckons, shaped by a moist wind
Through reflecting leaves to a cluster of berries.

XIII

A boulder moves, it is a brown bear
Stretching claws in the speckling dawn-light.
The kingfisher shifts in his tree, untucks
His head from a wing. Peepers chitter;

Aspens flutter tinsel leaves.
Beneath the mist-drift, ruffled water
Sips at the shore stones; an otter,
Bead eyes brazen with fresh hunger,
Thrusts up from a water hole.

XIV

Leaning inward, you float lips of roses
In a shallow bowl, smoothing the stain
On the white tablecloth, setting
New candles in the candelabra.
Poised in the drift of their light, your mouth
Shifts darkening and shines clear. Loose hair
Shivers electric over your ear.

XV

In moist April, adder's tongue flickers yellow
Amid mottled leaves. Bloodroot, early in May,
Blossoms up through moss and mold,
White as a star, its tall stem brimming
With crimson juice. Through the whole summer,
Heal-all thrusts its fuzzy purple
Above the hectic weeds. Tangled
Bittersweet bears autumn berries
For the mother grouse. You and I
Searching private woods for wildflowers:
Jack-in-the-pulpit, dewdrops, forget-me-nots.

XVI

Behind the raspberry bramble, dappled by moonlight,
Your nipples, your dark hutch of hair. Overhead,
A coasting owl dangled a mouse tail
From its bill. And falling asleep,
Your eyes, swooning beyond me, rested where
A farm lake, haunted by hemlocks, glimmered
With swans paddling in slow circles
As the sprung fish in the center
Sailed out silver in crescent arcs.

XVII

By the weather vane, two owls—whiter
Than swans in the willow pond below—
Crick their heads back and forth in the moon-sheen:
One for you and one for me and—stepping
Out of sleep and behind the one for you
Or in front of the one for me—a third.
Swan wings scatter the willow-sky
In the flat pond water; the swans drift
Above the slatted, rain-gray fence,
Hover like smoke over the peeling barn,
Waft back across the oak-reflecting windows
Where leaves turn into quilts; then
Up again behind the moon and around—
The swans land dark as owls where two owls stood,
A shade between the one for you
And the one for me. Their bone bills
Touch, moonlight flutters their wings,
The stretched boards of the barn bulge
Pushing like a loosened sea,
And three owls flap out white,
Twisting upward through thick water.

XVIII

Your breath sways on the pillow, your hair
Whispers over the undertow of sleep,
Loosening like the swirl of seaweed
Writhing to awake. Shall I wake you?

XIX

Flipping downward, tail pulsing the waves,
His great flukes winging slowly, then slapping,
Pounding a stream of spray, he coasts to her,
Caresses her, backs off and dives, bursts up
Full into the air, rolls over on her,
Clasping her to him with both flippers;
Bobbing by her side, he sighs from his belly,
Steady in the ebb of the rocking tide.

You Hold Me in My Life

You hold me in my life you breathe my breath
My fingertips ignite within your shade
Within your shade there flares my little death
Whose held unmaking holds what you have made

Flesh of my flesh we kindle to a choice
It is a stone a cell of blood a child
Its voice is rising burning in your voice
And sings within my throat a little while

Bone of my bone you hold me in my flame
I am a burning voice a child a stone
Within your cell I sing our own child's name
And as he rises I lie down alone

Alone my body and my world with you
We leave our blessing though all deaths burn true

Welcoming Poem
for the Birth of My Son

Bubbling and bouncing, lumbering amid
The tickle of little fishes, whales
Jostle the sea; they are blubber balloons
Sailing their bodies' happiness, spouting
Hallelujah to the surmise of seals,
The memoranda of walruses, while
In the daft radiance of arctic noon,
Emperor penguins gather, for whom, as always,
It is opening night.

Again, this blazing noon,
The play begins: reindeer grazing eastward
Raise their dazed eyes, jaws in their poised heads
Sluicing lichen juices; they gaze beyond hunger
In first wonder of wet light, dreaming
What is there, while whales are blooming,
While walruses are making lists for Christmas
And penguins parade new clothes through meadows
Of the white garden.

Up from the horizon,
Humped with porpoises; over the frozen sea
Where whales' bodies are blossoming games;
Past walruses puckered to blow kisses,
Whiskered like Santa Claus; to the applause
Of seals fanning with their flippers the hot glaciers
In the zeal of their unbounded, bounding hearts—
He comes, all spirit, dressed in flesh and blood;
He comes, crowned in his ears and fuzz,
In a dazzle of fingers and toes, making
Miracles with his glad eyes;
He walks in the sun-struck kingdom of penguins
Enraptured on their eggs, crying GOOD WILL
To that angered city where my love hides.

from
Guarded by Women (1963)

In a Field

Here, in a field
Of devil's paintbrushes,
The circle of far trees
Tightens, and near bushes
Hump like ruins
When the moon floats loosely
Past the desolation
Owl moans wake. Here,
As if the world's
Last lovers, we
Have rung from the ruins
The whippoorwill's
Thrust of melody.
You have fallen asleep,
Breathing as the wind breathes
Among wetted thistle,
The scented vine,
And, listening, I move
My body toward you,
When a small convulsion
Shakes your hand,
The moonlight flashes
On your teeth.
I am afraid to kiss you.
Never have I wished more
Not to die.

Descending

It is all falling away, the days fall faster now;
There float the first two dried and curling leaves
Gathered by a wind into the emptiness
That only we are able to imagine,
The emptiness of ourselves and of our falling.
And having shaped the sorrows of my breath
Into the sorrow of autumnal elegy,
Why do I turn so suddenly it shakes my eyes,
Only to discover my own surprise
And the road narrowing over the hill behind me?

And have I known you in no other way
Beyond the cruelty that turned your lip,
Beyond the urgency whose dreams betray—
Of lovers rotting in their mutual grave
Whom no autumnal elegy can save,
Touching bone fingertip to fingertip?
It is all falling away, the emptiness
That held us reaching, always the same,
And the touch by which we turned apart;
And now, emptied even of blame,
There is only our falling and the leaves
Curled in the wind by the maple tree,
Scattering like choices that we made
That quivered with surprise as the road
Narrowed over the hill behind me.

Conceived in the spaceless womb,
Moving through emptiness thereafter,
What can I find but terror in the laughter
Of stars, knowing the trout cannot know
A drowning world, nor the mole,
His warm belly brushing through a hole,

Know that he desecrates a grave?
And the hawk, in his brave circling,
Will he not lift his eyes to see the sun?
And we, what more could we have done,
Before we kept in dispossession
The kisses that no mortal lips can keep
And the embrace that does not fall away
Into the passiveness of sleep?

Descending past the garden where the dead crow
Jangles on a stick; descending past
The graveyard where the bluebird prinks
In uncontemplative delight; down past the orchard
Where the cherry trees are hung with silver cups
To frighten off the bobolinks;
Down through the meadow where summer went,
The harvest's melancholy and the scythe's lament,
Only the falling sustains me, only the falling
Seems steady now, open as it is, and near,
Almost to touch, as the consummation that I fear
No man and woman can achieve or lack,
And perfect as the paradise whose gates—
Closing behind the hill of the road
That narrows behind me—beckon me back.

The Boat

I dressed my father in his little clothes,
Blue sailor suit, brass buttons on his coat.
He asked me where the running water goes.

"Down to the sea," I said; "Set it afloat!"
Beside the stream he bent and raised the sail,
Uncurled the string and launched the painted boat.

White birds, circling the mast, wrenched his eyes pale.
He leaped on the tight deck and took the wind.
I watched the ship foam lurching in the gale,

And cried, "Come back, you don't know what you'll find!"
He steered. The ship grew, reddening the sky
As waves throbbed back, blind stumbling after blind.

The storm receded in his darkened eyes,
And down he looked at me. A harbor rose.
I asked, "What happens, father, when you die?"

He told where all the running water goes,
And dressed me gently in my little clothes.

Neanderthal

The Neanderthals, 40,000 years ago . . . apparently cared solicitously for their sick and aged. At La Chapelle were the remains of a nearly toothless cripple who must have been kept alive by his fellows. They not only obtained food for him but must have prechewed it. —*New York Times*, 18 December 1961

Had he no God to die for, no heaven
To which his burly bones might rise,
That, so humbled, he should so hold on?

In hairy youth, had he no borders,
No hunting grounds, in whose name
Sacrifice upon his tongue was sweet?

Could that purposeless, vain vale of fears,
Without justice, abrupt beginning,
Abrupt into the grave, and nothing more,
Not mystery, but death—could that
Absurdity mean so much to him?

Mankind, where is your next place,
One last hope away, your gospelled eyes
Scorched into their last remorse, your lips
Babbling, "Apocalypse!" to shake
The justice from the skies?

My death—that's quite something else,
I can believe in that. Before sleep,
Too happy in an unhappy world, something
Grips inside, something pulls at my eyes,
Slips in the chambers of my ears
And in the sea pours; my tongue waves
Like a handerchief, GOODBYE, into the echo
Of the dark of 40,000 years.

Too long, too long to have been dead;
40,000 years and not yet resurrected.

Raw toothless gums, hold on, hold on!

Canoe Ride

The butterfly is racked upon the lake;
I do not slow my boat to help it out.
Along the shore the quaking aspens quake.
What is this windy evening all about?

Tangled dark in dark, the evergreens
Reflect the water, which reflects them back;
The early short-eared owl knows what this means
Who likes the way the brittle mouse bones crack.

And with him I enjoy his appetite
And share the crooked weasel's crooked chase,
Strained sleep by day, strained wariness by night,
With crow calls coming from an empty place.

Among the ferns the nervous peepers cry;
Racoons tonight will eat the scraps I leave;
I could have saved a single butterfly,
But chose to let the lilting water grieve.

Is cruelty redeemed by consciousness?
Compassion is an intellectual thing.
Is sorrow sung the final happiness?
Four lonely notes white-throated sparrows sing.

The Mountain

Almost—I came so close,
As if my understanding
Might have been the trees themselves.
The mountain, with the sun behind it,
Seemed across the lake no space away,
Almost like the closing of my eyes,
Near as all presences are near
By which one is reminded
Of oneself, being separated,
And, in isolation, almost understanding,
Coming so close. Liquid, the loon calls,
Over the water, spilled like memories
As they drift away, always
In their soft diminishing.

What is it you once told me?
Always my closeness seemed to change
What waited to be understood, but seeking it,
It moved away, and the distance
That remained I understood, remembering
I had forgotten you, forgotten
What you said, and that, too close,
You changed, dwindling away,
Even as the mountain changed,
Steaming in its underbrush decay
With mushrooms enchanted yellow and red,
And the dewy moth fluttering
In the splattered evergreen light.
Invisibly the mountain changed,
My closeness changing it somehow,
So that I could not see its transformation,
For I came too close,
Having almost understood.

Across the lake beyond pebbles warbling
And the loons' low water sounds,
The mountain is diminishing,
It is dwindling out of sight
As the last crow flies,
And a shadow from within
Draws me back closer to myself—
Dwindling in my own mountainous shade,
Forgetting, trying almost not to remember,
Almost welcoming the isolation,
And the dark, the dark, the dark.

Separation

Wet midnight grass chills my body
With a wakefulness beyond fatigue.
Behind me floats a silhouette of trees,
And before, hushed, spaceless in distance,
Spread to the limits of my vision—
The horizon of the Adirondack range.
Through the sky, the Northern Lights,
Vibrating ghostliness, stream upward
Toward a central point, above my head,
Which of itself is darkness; a glow appears,
A green haze, a falling pause, and then
A poverty of words with which to praise
Not merely what I see, but what I feel
I see, a poverty of words
To praise the wordless praise itself.
These are the thoughts I would write to you
As if the wordless mystery of things
Was what I sought, as if just talking to you
Were not, at this hour, all I wished.

South Beach

For eight summers we had walked here,
Thinking we had lasted it out, laughing
That having called it quits a hundred times
We were now safe, that even unhappiness
Had become a bond. Here once again
The gull's uplift and cry distracts me,
Rising above the cliff's September brush,
Goldenrod, and the treasonous ivy;
Here, without your knowing it, sun dazes,
Everything is light even to blankness,
The blank hope of the glinting shore
And the seashell sand from which no actual
Embarkation will be made. I have returned
Here by myself, trying to think things through,
But it is vain: there is no punishment
Humbly to endure, no judgment,
And yet, even without blame,
There is no forgiveness of oneself.

I have returned here by myself
Where, for eight years, you watched me
With the same three boyhood friends,
Playing stoop ball against a rock. And still
I tell myself that what was once possessed
Never can be lost, endings cannot undo
The past that they define, but it is vain,
It takes death to accept death,
And my living flesh contends against
The living sun, distracting me,
Though I am here to think things through.

Two children splash along this beach
As if this summer's day will have no end.

I lie back on my towel, cover my face
With the *New York Times*, and think things through
As the ocean rasps upon the shore
By the breaker where our dog was killed.
In the blown sand and the water's spray,
I tell myself that all is vanity,
Even accepting vanity is vain;
I do five extra push-ups, take a dip,
Relieved at last by the absence of hope,
And feel then, tightening on my lips,
The white, determined smile of the drowned.

Father

I have not needed you for thirteen years.
You left my mother to me like a bride.
To take your place, I shut off all my tears,
And with your death, it was my grief that died.
How could I know that women worship pain?
My mother's eyes bring back your ghost again.

    I dreamed that digging in the humid ground
    You found, among the worms, my embryo;
    You put it on a hook—it made no sound
    Opening its mouth as you let it go
    Into the lake where, fishing from a boat,
    You watched the bulging, blood-eyed fishes float.

Failing, the strong at last learn gentleness.
When you cried out—that was your mastery!
I took a wife, but never let her guess
It was your ghost that chose my secrecy.
She needed what you would not have me show:
My need. Your strength too late let weakness grow.

    I dreamed we both rowed through a windy mist;
    The dark lake tilted where you wished to go.
    Fish scales and blood glowed at me from your wrist;
    The air I gulped only the drowning know.
    You had me hold the net, and I believed
    The fish's spastic death was what I grieved.

Screams come too easily these guarded days;
The bright, complaining, are most eloquent.
Must loss always be prelude to our praise?
Is this what mother's rising mourning meant?
For whose sake did I envy suicide?
Could death win wife and mother as one bride?

I dreamed you threw the unhooked fish away.
Why did I fear I had done something wrong?
You took me home, insisting that I stay,
But I did not feel weak, feeling you strong.
With nothing said, you left the net behind
To anger the gored waters of my mind.

I have not needed you for thirteen years.
I have grown grim with my authority.
Take back my mother and release my tears,
And let a child's lost grief give strength to me!
    Dreaming, I seek your skeleton below;
    I dig the worms and find your embryo.

Grieving on a Grand Scale

Wailing its burst mechanical heart,
The plane plunged between two hills,
And you were dead. I day-dreamed that.
How could I mourn you if you really died?
And how, dear one, can I truly grieve
For the plain girl raped in Central Park,
Her mouth shaped like a grave; the boy by the truck,
Only bicycle wheels still spinning;
For the old man with nothing to do;
For the fox, one summer dead, flies
Strumming the revealed harp of his chest;
For birds, killed by insecticides;
For the bugs? Should they be mourned too?
And for those who will die in wars to come,
How shall I mourn that abstraction? And how
Can I guard against pitying myself
When to die is to go where no hot women,
Twisted into hands and hair,
Greet one with gratifying tears?

O, not to hate because grieving fails,
Because sorrow shudders merely into art,
But to mourn softly, without hope of resurrection,
As, through rainy memory, my hands
Rise to take off your clothes, and faraway,
Still before dawn, the scent of munched pears
Follows the first wind where young deer
Do not move as their loose watery lips
Slide over their gums with a sound like weeping.

Adam on His Way Home

Three crows by the wayside sat on a cross.
The journey back was long, the rank road
Passable only on foot, and his memories
Were little consolation. What good was past

Happiness, or, for that matter, past
Suffering? In these limp days, dignity
Was poor payment for leaky eyes. Nothing
Could be set against death as in old times.

The buzzard sun flapped in his face, rattling
His wrists, his elbows, his ribs, as a tide
Of ocean pebbles mumbled in his ears,
"Nothing, nothing." Over his toes lizards

Ran where nails cracked and peeled. And this
Was not the mud of penitence, but decay;
This was the limp time, with cramped air clotted
In his nose, his tongue shrivelled dry as rope.

And then, although he was not superstitious,
It happened, as he always knew it would.
Beneath the apple tree, a draped figure,
Featureless, shaped as if by wind on water,

Drew him down whispering, "Come to me,
I am the one!" His breath parted the wind,
Like clothes fallen away, and there she lay
Smiling with his young eyes and his fierce tongue

With its lying power. He breathed apart
Her foaming water-thighs which clutched the dark,
His own, his calling dark, smelling of home,
Where he leapt in the final spasm of first love.

The Shooting

I shot an otter because I had a gun;
The gun was loaned to me, you understand.
Perhaps I shot it merely for the fun.
Must everything have meaning and be planned?

Afterwards I suffered penitence,
And dreamed my dachshund died, convulsed in fright.
They look alike, but that's coincidence.
Within one week my dream was proven right.

At first I thought its death significant
As punishment for what I'd lightly done;
But good sense said I'd nothing to repent,
That it is natural to hunt for fun.

Was I unnatural to feel remorse?
I mourned the otter and my dog as one.
But superstition would not guide my course;
To prove that I was free I bought the gun.

I dreamed I watched my frightened brother die.
Such fancy worried me, I must admit.
But at his funeral I would not cry,
Certain that I was not to blame for it.

I gave my friend the gun because of guilt,
And feared then what my sanity had done.
On fear, he said, the myth of hell was built.
He shot an otter because he had a gun.

Resurrection

Upon the shore, the bleached skull,
More regular than stone, glistens—
A cast-away, abandoned sun
Among planetary pebbles, galaxies of sand.
Dragged out again to drown as aged gulls
Gossip its descent, the skull's sockets
Suck the foam with the crooked teeth
Sighing sea-weed from the deep sea-dunes.

A skeleton rises erect in the moonlight
Like clouds clustered into shape;
There to the south, outstretched, float
Delicate finger-bones; to the north,
His cupped right palm catches feathers
Fallen from angel-wings. Thigh-bones,
Knee-bones, ankle-bones, toes, dangle in place,
Yet all are jointed, all held intact.

He floats swiftly now to the west, as if
Summoned, as if dreaming himself
Unencumbered up through space,
Without a tongue, without a voice.
The sea sparkles with the living sperm
Of his once-loved, rejected light.

The Compact

Jack sat upon his mother's widowed bed;
Though rumpled moist from sleep, the sheets were clean.
Without consent from Jack she would not wed.
Choosing for her a choice he could not mean,
Jack walked his dog; the cool air warmed his head.
Achieved unselfishness earned him her praise;
Her gratitude taught him a lover's ways.

Jack's marriage hid his old fidelity.
The Jill Jack loved too soon, soon found that out:
She hoped their love would someday set Jack free,
But felt safe that this never came about.
When Jack's dog wet the rug he spanked it gently.
Jack organized his desk before he read,
And combed his hair before he went to bed.

His wounded Jill, how could she ever tell
What love would do when love got in the way?
Jack's recent father tried to love Jack well;
Jack felt true gratitude, and yet one day
He shot a beaver cleanly through the skull.
Jack rocked his dog that midnight like a child,
And this one time his Jill smiled when he smiled.

When lovers love according to their wound,
A discord sharpens in that harmony.
Inside that room the two of them were bound.
Jill dreamed Jack's mother's dog snarled angrily.
Jack dreamed his dog was dug out of the ground.
"You're one of us," was what his mother said
When at Jill's wedding all of them were wed.

Jill loved Jack in a blunt, hurt child's way,
Clothing herself in pain to be his bride.
Jack's dog was run down on a summer's day,
And when he cried, his father's ghost replied:
"Who love the living must the dead betray."
Jill left the room with Jack still faithful there,
Mourning dead love beyond love's last repair.

The Stairs

for My Mother

I

 White, pointed shoes and ankles trimmed
By morning shade, she is stepping down
The stairs on my father's holiday
In the fuss and flutter of her dress;
And we are waiting for her, queen
Of sandwiches and admonishments.

 On the walnut table by the window,
Green grapes, each with an eye of light,
Rest beside the punched cigar box
Which keeps the toads and salamanders,
The praying mantis and the Indian pipes,
That I will capture on this day —
As we wait for her, stepping down
The sunday stairs my father's morning.

 And on this day that lasted out
The summertime my father's woods
Rang out our ringalievio,
There by the window, pooled in sun,
In my turtleneck red sweater,
Stands my sister; I am supposed
To take her with me, and, knowing I will,
I tell her No, that girls get eaten
In the pine grove by the giant's cave.

 This day's goodnight: a puppet show
For which we kept ourselves awake
By a pavilion where the lake
Smeared moonlight with the lantern-glow
White as her pointed shoes stepping

Down the stairs as we wait for her
This holiday morning, this long sunday
Of my father's summertime.

II

      Your husband, mother, is long dead.
Here in the shade of this twisted tree,
I watch geese rise from the lake, white throats
Thrust out in a fanfare of startled wings.
If ever I am a father, may my children
Inherit this stilled, white hour, recalling
At the top of the stairs, as I do now,
Someone I love descending to them.

Splitting Firewood

Up from my belly, up from my back,
The swinging blood floods in my arms,
Locks my elbows flat; my fingers grip
Against the grim smack of the axe
As the thud, the wood's recoil and clap
Echoes out into the wide weather
Of the windy afternoon.

My cheeks puff with not quite yet
Spent breath; the little nut of air
Grows in an instant in my lungs
Into an oak, into my raised axe that cries
"Again, again" in a bugle call of joys.
Yes, here I am, my axe, my tree of breath,
Flames in my hair, my hands, flames
In my back and in my belly's hearth.

And there is the piled wood,
And the defied wind,
And the boulders behind the apple trees
Grey in the sun's descent,
And the mirror of ice,
The sky in the mirror,
And the afternoon over.

I place one last log on the grate
As from the chimney night wind sucks
At our fireplace. Warm together
In our bed, I hear my curled wife
Whimper in her sleep.

Song for Patricia While Cat-Napping on the Beach

Thinning into space, blue air,
And on the shore, junk of the sea:
Lobster claws, mussel shells, anemone,
As clouds curl like a waiting cat
Whose eye blinks open to a stare
That shines upon me standing there,
Watching me appear within your sight.
My disbelieving mind delights
In dreaming forms I may become
Where in the sun-cat's eye I am,
Being happy, being here,
Out of the experimenting sea,
Beginning my first human year,
With your real light now entering me.

Raking Leaves

Packed with woodpeckers, my head knocks,
Coaxing the bark of the tree to make its sap speak—
My sap, my boned branches, my veined leaves
Staining the wind, dizzying down
Amid a busyness of birds.

And in the bedroom, flushed hands warm with work,
She smoothes the wrinkles from the sheets
That last night's tumbled sleep may once again
Grow young, that habit, fondled back
Into desire, may heat the holy place
Where flesh is sung. And unknown even
To herself—who does not live by words—
She dreams this place again, again,
Whose branches are the memories of birds;
She eases drifting through a noon of bells
Replenishing her purpose to return,
With no debts in her comings or farewells.

Raking, quickly taking time in the nick,
I watch my feet glide through the ragged shade
Of the shagbark hickory, burly in the blood
Of my own speed, my own strength, now smack
In the sun, savagely bright, sight
For closed eyes; and up, out again to seek,
I take, I make what I will, skill of delight
I am not author of; above, no missing God I miss;
High satisfying sky though, and below,
Chrysanthemums in garb of gaiety,
Little serious clowns; and look, beyond the brook
The fat grouse bumps across the field
And jumps for berries in the honeysuckle.

Not here, not now, one world goes down,
And, not in my head, the serious men
Chronicle its going; I cannot tell them
I am raking leaves. This day is hers,
This is my time; with us together
Two chores away, all rocking hours support
This hour, all knocking days repeat this day.

from
A Stranger's Privilege (1959)

Poem for You

Always have these clear sounds been in your ears:
The goat's clatter climbing across the wall
To reach the olive branch where leaves flash, dartin
Like fishes, silver and green. Always you hear
The voice of morning and afternoon's long call
Of open air, the whip of evening smarting
The sky and herding in slow clouds like sheep
Over the horizon's hill—simple,
Simple as the taste of bread, simple as sleep,
And far away, farther than mountain people
In little white towns, dreaming chores of butter,
Milk and hay, without a cause to utter,
Without a dream within a dream reversing
Dreams away. And always in your eyes
Are shadows, blue and amber, interweaving,
And fabrics of bright grasses and rough skies,
While hunter and the frozen hare assemble,
While pinecones drop and all the forests shudder,
Though death is simple to the forest people;
And on the moss the orange salamander
Is like a wink of daylight, time's reminder
That nothing ends and nothing really matters
Except to you, except to you. Wind grew
With rain to shake the scarecrow into tatters—
And nothing really matters, except to you.
And always your hands learn, always your touch
Tells the season in the stone or branch
With weather's words, with wet, with shivering,
And tells a tale of underwater people
Whose tides are like your own; like you they sing
All comings and all goings are so simple:
Nothing to take with us, nothing to bring.
You have not ever known that air can smother
Or that it is a foreign element,

That what you hear and see and touch together
Is never what you feel or what is meant,
That nothing ends and nothing really matters,
That what you love is always almost true.
Wind grew to shake the scarecrow into tatters,
And nothing really matters, except to you.

Fiesole, 1957

Arrivals

Here comes, with those occurrences of mind,
Perhaps some rain, some snow, perhaps some sun,
Clouds shaped by thoughts that once were left behind,
Come you, come I, now see, comes everyone.
And these arrivals are not ever done;
Events dance purely for that secret sight
When all the candles of the heart are gone,
And gone, in time, the candles of delight.
But if I still delay, now I've begun
To love you with nostalgia of the rain,
Shyness of snow, possessiveness of sun,
Remember—candles to the touch are pain;
What minds conceive cannot be purely done,
Though here come you, come I, comes everyone.

Parable

Within the introspection of my dying
I reversed myself in the darkness of indecision
Because of all that hatred:
Anger of birds—their shrill philosophy,
Fish uncaring and cold in their own blood,
And animals who would not talk with me.
And I wiped the honey from my jaw with the paw
Of my hand, and I said to the quarrelsome birds: beware,
The fox will find your nest and devour your eggs;
And I said to the meditative fish: beware,
The carefree otter will spear you in the foam,
And to the arty beaver, the snobbish deer,
The arrogant porcupine, I said: beware
The season when leaves and flowers bloom dry
And the bark of the tree is acid to your tongue,
But they did not reply,
And I reversed myself in the darkness of indecision.
This was the first warning, the elemental cry,
And I started back from where I came
Where waters fountained once in happiness,
The mothering season cradling me secure,
But now the trees were clothed in funereal light,
And insects heckled me out of the grass.
This was the second warning, the strangeness,
And I reversed myself
Within the introspection of my dying.
And the first and second warnings sounded
In my ears like waves, like crumbling crags,
And I turned to the heedless animals and said:
It is not bad to feel you are alone,
But bad that no one's company consoles;
It is not bad to feel that you are lost,
But bad to think there is no place to go

Beyond the darkness of your indecision.
And this third warning I told the animals,
But they did not reply.
Within the darkness of my indecision,
Within the introspection of my dying,
I stopped still as I could and did not move,
And the animals came forth and licked my hands.

Anecdote of the Sparrow

The modern house, with its window eye,
Stared like an idol at the sun.
Such judgment singed the air that one
Could almost hear the flowers cry
Down in the garden below the glass
Where the broken sparrow lay.
What silent force will block the way
Or smash us as we try to pass
On some bright noon to seek our place?
Prepare, since even gods are blind,
For things unseen. Make yourself kind
Before the glass reveals your face!

The Other Lives

She could not be his—too much required change;
Her world beckoned him back into the past
Where clay cliffs split and slid into the sea.
Having killed the fear of death, he would not
Relinquish willingly a single breath,
And wished to share with her his sense of woods
In which his father's voice cried in the wind,
In which the lake at twilight answered the loon
To say another misted day is gone.
He leaned to her, for he would tell her this—
That there was nothing they could ever share
Except this knowledge, nothing but a moment
Echoing across the wistful country
Of all that could not be. Woodcock warblings
From an ancient sleepiness softly gave out
Upon the patient listening of the lake,
And on pine needles she reclined her head.
Through hemlock shade slant sun revealed the dust
Before his eyes; dust filled the parent air
And rested on his hands. There was not breath
Enough to make the endless explanations;
Not enough breath, and dust was falling dry
Upon his lips, and she would turn to him
Only in murmurings of other worlds.

The Monster Who
Loved the Hero

I met a monster in a wood:
"It's not my fault!" choked through her cries,
Blowing her blue nose loud as she could,
Tears pouring from her bloodshot eyes.

Being practised in the art,
I raised my lance to poke her through;
But I could not play out my part—
Hers was no strategy I knew.

"The ugliest need love the most,
And if you take me home with you,
You'll find at last someone to trust,
For beauty never could be true."

Such fine sentiment made me pause,
Though she was not my type one bit;
It seemed against my whole life's cause
To find love and not pity it.

She saw me weaken, and she smiled.
I swear she gloated in her grin.
I must confess, that got me riled:
I took my lance and did her in.

To the Lover
Haunted by His Vow

Hate that kingdom where restlessness is stilled,
Where longing seeks out love to find release,
Where lions play with lambs like any child,
And enemies together banquet in peace!

That is the grave—it is no place to go.
Turn inward where the torturer is found;
Thank your enemy when he strikes his blow,
And let the boar sing praises to the hound.

Then take her though the cowards moralize,
Though good friends are embarrassed, parents faint,
Though judges gossip in their legal guise;
Defy all laws and suffer no restraint.

And let this be your epitaph: He moved,
Among these cities and those hills, sublime,
For what he knew was dead he would not love,
And each love was immortal in its time.

The Rumor

I   The Conversation

Have you heard the rumors of black water lying
Where tongues of bloated cattle are twisted by ants,
Rumors of rotten wheat and locusts dying,
And prophets whipped, mocked by children's chants?
The only innocence they know is pain.
And echoed by the dark symposium
Of crows, filling the sky with thoughts of rain,
Heat thickens and again the rumors come,
Rumors from the governor's estate
Of boasted incest, of prolonged revenge,
A young girl stoned to death by the north gate.
Some thought that she was raped—but who can judge?
The dutiful men, having left the jury,
Shuddering with hidden fears of death,
Find freedom only in adultery,
In breaking bonds that are the gift of breath;
The only love they feel is clandestine,
Mistaking the forbidden for the intense,
But I know secretly just what they mean
And wish to master that same violence.
I spread these rumors as I talk to you,
And don't believe the very words I speak,
But even if I did, what could I do?
The rumors tell of rain within a week.
And have you heard, some crazy bastard hammers
In the red sun and hammers in the dark;
Muttering of doom and floods, he stammers
To his sons, and builds himself an ark.

II   The Drowning and Last Dream

O Lord, what will you do when I am gone,
When this spinning green world is grayly washed

217

And purged away? Let your final tear fall
In the absurdity of your concern
And flood the mortal hill with its salt blessing.
For now, cleansed of ambition and remorse,
Weightless, without the body's hope, I know
Myself to be the breathing of your care,
The testament of your great loneliness.
And now I pity you who supervise
My death, guilty even in your just wrath,
While beyond your pained nostalgia I escape
Into that sweet oblivion you cannot choose.
Your waters rock me out of fear, and rock
Away the vanity of worshipping
Posterity—nations and cities—as if
The dust of brick filled more than empty time.
Now history is gone, now earth dissolves
To seas, and seas to skies, and skies contract
Into your memory where the white eagle
Always hovers and glides and kingfishers plunge
For salmon in the studded lake; always
The congregation of the caribou
Makes holy the hour of thirst while proud pharoah
Meditates upon his masterpiece,
And in the desert of my drowning mind
Moses hears a voice that speaks in fire
Beyond the waters of this final sea.
Will he survive, O Lord, in spite of me?

A Song for Eve

Sweetly let considerations go;
Let wisdom wonder at the alphabet;
Let pears and plums and peaches fall like snow.
"Adam, do you taste the apple yet?"

Swiftly let our speculations flee.
Sun mellows on your arms, your eyes are wet,
And some new breathlessness floods filling me.
"Adam, do you taste the apple yet?"

Sharply let recriminations come;
To lose a world is something to regret,
Although your tears make former love seem dumb.
"Adam, do you taste the apple yet?"

Sweetly, swiftly, sharply, all love goes;
And what the fateful apple is, Eve knows.

The Fall

And when I opened up my eyes I saw
The dawn light frost the apple tree;
I stepped out of the dream of the sea
Into the separated sky,
And walked the new-made glittering grass
Past golden peach and nectarine.
The dream of the sea moved in my mind
With its multitude of fishes, currents of whales,
And so at my waking I found her by my side.
What thankfulness and what unease,
To wake and find a dream grown true,
And I spun in a vertigo
Of happenings not yet come,
And settled where the universe began.
In the beginning, I stirred in a dream
Of the chaos of empty winds, chaos
Of dark upon dark motion, but I saw
In the unreal waiting a past eternally gone,
Though when I opened up my eyes I watched
The dawn light frost the apple tree.
The beginning, the separated heavens,
The sea, the land and the innocence of animals—
Here in the garden as it had to be,
Waiting as in a memory
That draws you back within a dream,
And you wake to find the memory is true,
And the dream is what must come to be,
Fixed and waiting as in a memory.
And so at my waking I found her
By my side, true as she had to be,
True as the miracle of sky and birds,
True as the water's blessing, the pensive oak,
The graceful birch, and the frolic of squirrels

In a frolic of leaves—all dancing
Through the new-made light, and, in the center,
I opened my eyes and watched
The dawn light frost the apple tree.
And my dreaming mind conceived
The jealous blow and the tide of blood
Gathering to the sorrow of waters,
Animals, two by two, again
The monotony of peace, again the unheard cry,
And the ultimate anger of the fire—
Because of the beginning. And I remember
She was gone, and I knew why, and even though
It was a dream, I ran, hoping to stop her,
Trying to wake before the beginning;
And there, eyes closed, we lay together,
Remembering it did not have to be.
I opened up my eyes and watched
The dawn light frost the apple tree.

My Shadow Rides

My shadow rides the windless air;
I listen, wrapped in animal dark,
Where silver fishes, waved in fear,
Flee barracuda and the shark,
Where tracking through the snowy wood,
The single-minded wolverine
And lynx, dressed gaudily in rabbit blood,
Lick themselves clean.

Like organ pipes the booming sun
Blasts sleepy birds into the air,
And on the waves Leviathan
Dances his oceanic care,
And deer drink honey from the dew,
And beavers build in brotherhood;
And even if this all were true,
Would it be good?

In animal dark I sing this song
To forest of eye and ocean of ear;
And what is right and what is wrong
Are not unfolded here.

Dialogue in Perversity

Because she fears he might in time succeed,
She stays with him; failure binds him to her,
And fear always holds them where they were.
How then can we define her smallest deed,
Arranging jonquils in a shaded room,
Or understand his progress to the tomb,
When his own test, in truth, his greatest need,
Is proving he can beautifully lose?
Then is perversity the way they choose?

"I hurt you from the heart, from jealousy,"
She says, "am secret, angry out of need,
And cannot help but sow a bitter seed."
"Your will," he says, "must take on mastery."
Such weakness brings her to a consciousness
That makes her more; why should it make him less?
And is his strength then his perversity?
No blood spills at the dying of a word.
She says, "Here where I am you feel the cold."

Some overcome their needs, and some give in;
But which of these is true perversity?
What swift reversal in one's mastery
Makes it attendant on the biding sin?
She carries in the meat, the bread, olives,
Ripe tomatoes, wine—for which he gives
Her thanks, and turns to face his thoughts again.
"All will," he says, "depends on opposition,
And thought itself confirms this contradiction."

Black are the streets, the windows, earth and sky.
In blackness does philosophy begin;
It ends by letting further blackness in

By adding to the many ways we die.
And is all their perversity perverse?
They grow together as their lives grow worse.
She says, "It takes some honesty to lie."
"Yet consciousness is not an end," says he.
And they are circling through eternity.

In the Waking

In the waking of my eye
The ringing winter world runs white,
Two cardinals are points of light,
An icicle reflects the sky,
And snow-carved pines curve into sight.

But now the whiteness starts to blind,
And through a dark transparency
The winter morning murmury
With worlds to come wakes in my mind
A thought of you whose thought is me.

I cannot love myself alone,
Yet see you watching me apart,
And all my eye's spontaneous art
Is still as icicle and stone
And timeless as this planet's start.

You are the one I single out
To rouse my passive eye to dance
And make a choice where all is chance—
Of stars exploding in the night
Whose lost lights endlessly advance.

A Letter from Hell

Dear friend, there are no lakes of fire here,
No chains of ice, no boulders to be pushed
Up mountainsides, but fiends race through my mind,
Naked, distorting sleep. And when I'm flushed
With dreams of you as we in harvest pluck
Red apples in a holiday of snow,
I fall to wake so sorrowfully wise,
For by the vividness of loss we know
The place we've left, the truth of words we've said,
And mourn the richness of mahogany
That framed the fiery roast, the heartfelt bread.
The plum, once tasted, waters in my mouth,
And in my cheek, with an autumnal sound,
The plum pit softly sings a dying round;
Dying, not death, defines our punishment.
And change is all the sorrow we can know;
Home is the place from where we always go.

My torture is the farewell wail of wind;
This summer's butterfly is not the same—
The likeness pains—I am not fooled, but I
Pretend and call it still by last year's name.
A rude rush gathers in the streets I walk,
And moving with the crowd I know a dread
Of oceans sounding sibilants like talk.
Plaster crumbles in houses of the poor;
Beneath the floor the rats grow plump, and children
Feel them gnawing at their bones. The rich
Are stiff but tired and push away their food,
No sensual consolation does them good,
While we whose pride is in our libraries
Will study late to cram a prisoned head,
And lie about the books we have not read.
But sometimes in the pauses of the dark,

Or in the woods between the thrush's song
And bluejay's cry, it seems that I belong
Beyond myself, I feel within the air
The thunder's pulse, a breathing everywhere,
And then my lips go dumb, my doubt is shame,
And still beyond myself, beyond my fear,
I sense that there is something holy there.

 Of course, this passes, I turn to what I know —
The girls, I love them all, anonymous
In loveliness; what else is there to do?
And when the moon is frozen in my eye
I touch them with a meaning that is true.
But there is not a day that they can keep;
What can they want of me? I only leave them
In the flesh, and yet they weep, they weep.
And I have seen upon the softest bed
Their hair turned rough as grass, their look
Dissolved into a slime, their aching arms
A skeleton to hug a stone. What god
Shaped ancient nothingness into these scenes?
If you can hear, my friend, speak out the truth,
Reveal the end of evil through the means!

 I write these words out for myself, dear friend,
For you are gone into a foreign weather,
And find I feel no loss despite this end;
It is enough we met and talked together.
It is enough you stirred me into song
And cheered me when the black rains broke behind me,
And made me sad when sunshine strode too long,
Reminded of the browning leaves before me.
Now you have gone into a foreign weather,
And leave me with a sadness of my own
I could not share were we again together;
It is enough I find that I have grown.
I write these words out for myself, dear friend;
Heaven will not begin when hell will end.

The Departure

You had expected more. Now that I leave,
Fatigued with masterful pretense and doubt,
Again in me your empty life will thrive,
And once again you'll flourish as you grieve;
And all the while, so you may not find out,
I'll do the things that tied-down people talk about.

You had expected more, but found that giving
Was neither end nor was it consolation,
And learned the dead do not release the living,
Nor is there honesty in self-forgiving.
And when a mother fills and bears a son,
She passes on the crime by which all loving's done.

Again, as to a dream, you turn to me,
And I will go where I have never been
And see the things that you will never see
(Though nothing's new beyond its novelty).
But in my letters all will sound serene,
And comfort you with meanings that I do not mean.

I lie, and do you lie when you believe?
I fear that first dependency returns.
I look to you to look to me, and give
Those things alone that I cannot receive.
My friends say you look tired, but who discerns
That we will lie together when the whole world burns?

Your hands have paled to a transparency,
There are the veins, the bones—how very thin,
How smooth they are, how cool, when they touch me
I feel the rocking of my infancy.
I lie, I lie, for both our deaths begin,
And you are old without, and I am old within.

Again you turn to me, as to a dream.
Dream, dream, for the time of dreaming is not gone!
Though we are guilty of the oldest crime,
It yet may be transformed within a dream:
Who wakes beyond this nightmare loves all men,
Though wakening, you'll be expecting dreams again.

An Echo Sonnet to an Empty Page

Voice:	Echo:
How from emptiness can I make a start?	Start
And starting, must I master joy or grief?	Grief
But is there consolation in the heart?	Art
O cold reprieve, where's natural relief?	Leaf
Leaf blooms, burns red before delighted eyes.	Dies
Here beauty makes of dying, ecstasy.	See
Yet what's the end of our life's long disease?	Ease
If death is not, who is my enemy?	Me
Then are you glad that I must end in sleep?	Leap
I'd leap into the dark if dark were true.	True
And in that night would you rejoice or weep?	Weep
What contradiction makes you take this view?	You
I feel your calling leads me where I go,	Go
But whether happiness is there, you know.	No

The Doppelgänger

Down that still street where I have never passed,
No iron gateway whistles the slant winds,
No craze of moonlight crusts the steeple-glass,
No mute policeman muffles through his rounds.

My footfalls in her hall were never known
And never took the breathless, steep ascent;
The moment never came, has never gone.
There was no disappointment, no intent.

No owl puckered for its night-long note;
No squinty bats crooked through their jagged race.
At her address there was no one to dote
On the sick moon, my sorrows in his face.

He was not there and did not curse her house
Or thin his lips, and so he never said:
I live within another consciousness;
Where I am not, I waken from the dead.

The Appointment

I

What can she tell him now, does she even know
The actual hour was there to contain her wish
Now that even memory is composed,
Now that the knife is silent in the dish?
And can she take his hand, hoping that touch
Once more will sweep away the other lives
That always part them? She does not ask for much
Whose days will soon be buried in one grave
Of reveries as shadows take their place.
And if she rests her head, closing her eyes,
She has no single image of his face;
Her mind will wander through a thousand lies
To fix upon a scene she had forgotten.
Why recollect one day and not another:
The turtle floating in the bowl, all rotten,
The rapid waxy fingers of her mother?
Where is she now, to what can she return,
To what advance? The goal toward which her youth
Once seemed to point, she meditates to learn,
Is where, is past? Did it exist in truth?
She cannot think how she would change her life.
Whoever he may be, she is his wife.

II

Before her simplest hope, before her wish
Were chronicled in words and gesturings,
Before the knife was silent in the dish
And unfulfillment questioned all fulfillings,
Could she have known how promises repent,

That they are cruellest when they are not broken,
That expectation flattens the event?
Who's not rehearsed the tender words he's spoken?
She can remember Christmas toys her brother
Opened with delight, when, without reason,
She cried beside the Christmas tree as Mother
Told her Christmas is a happy season.
Always dissatisfied with satisfaction,
Always discontent with what she did
And discontent with her dissatisfaction,
Always eager, hopeful, disappointed,
Could she have told him: love me just a little,
Be cold, because to coldness we must come,
Be guarded, uncommitted, practical,
For faith returns you to your father's tomb?
But moonlit clouds and summer twilight moved
Their lips to say the words: how much they loved.

III

And looking back—when her own history
Shall seem to her that it was always there,
Shall seem at last, impersonal—will she
Remember bobolink and tanager
Across the stream, and yet forget the day
She watched, recall the sunfish strike the foam,
Stop still, then strike again and dart away,
And fail to place these images in time?
Will she remember dawn beside the lake
Before the wind came up, before round noon
Rose out and sat hard on the mountain's back,
Before the evening clamored on the stone,
When deer were watching her and broke their stare—
White tails, like fingers, warning not to follow—
And think what happens happens everywhere,
And think remembered deer are running now?
Will she then say to him that disappointment,
Love, and expectation all are one
And when love finds its circular intent
Then disappointment turns to expectation?
Sad are the farms where rain is not enough;
Sad is the lived, and sad the unlived life.

IV

Listen to me beyond my disappointment!
The vanished hour appears, still in a wish.
That brittle sound's a knife upon a dish.
In loving her, I gained the love I spent;
I keep that lost appointment now as one I meant.

Apocalypse

The angry hand touches our world,
And we whisper to each other:
Another second ends us.
Shall there be fire first, even the fish
Burned back into the rock, and afterward
The covering sea, the carved moon
And dispassionate stars shining
With no tree's shadow on the moss?
Another second ends us.
But we do not believe the words
Our own lips speak, do not believe our nerves
That will not let us sleep. The hare
Dreads the snapping twig, porcupines
Bristle at a sudden wind, dazed moose
Stomp through the woods while overhead
Geese honk and the marsh is muddy
From their turbulence. A second more—
Is it not now? Has not the poison finger
Turned the ripe fruit black, the crouching fire
Sprung up, and water swollen
Like a bloated fish?—A second more! Not yet?
And now I know there cannot be
The soft repose of hopelessness,
Only this uncertainty.

from
The Irony of Joy (1955)

Trying to Wake from
an Afternoon Dream
in Which My Teacher Dies

I am afraid, now I have seen who dies,
That I may come to fill the space
Of your authority, and find my face
Without new deepness in my eyes.

For I had been content to strive,
Imagining the sky's still blue
Around your head, a statue moving through
Its history. Your life made me alive.

Now the beating quickens in my heart,
And I am changed. The sun has pressed
Your shadows in my eyes—I take your part.
Wake me, let me not dream the rest!

A Cage in Search of a Bird

My destiny is not my own
Said the cage in search of a bird.
I am defined by what I do,
And when I'm empty, I'm absurd.

So I will find a willing bird
Who knows the limit of the skies
With wings that feel the chain his song
Must hold him in until he dies.

And he will make my bars his home
Beyond all vistas of the air,
And sing his song to me alone
Inside the echoes of despair.

And if some other bird should stop
When flying south to look and spin
About and say, "You can't get out,"
He would reply, "You can't get in."

A Bird in Search of a Cage

Said the bird in search of a cage:
This world is even large for wings,
The mindless seasons drive me down,
Tormenting me with changing things.

A cage is not escape, but need,
And though once in all travel's done,
I'll sing so every bird will know
My wanderings in moon and sun,

And all the crickets will be stilled,
And stilled the summer air and grass,
And hushed the secrets of the wind,
For when my final callings pass.

And if a friend should stop to talk,
Reminding me of what is past,
And ask the meaning of my song,
I'd say that only cages last.

The Way We Wonder

What has become of our astonishment
For simple things: color and the touch of day?
We wonder, now our early gift is spent,

About abstracted reasons to repent
For joy, blank words we've heard our parents say.
What has become of our astonishment

For night and space, for stars we can't invent?
(While crickets tick the perfect night away.)
We wonder, now our early gift is spent,

Whether some miraculous event
Will soon reveal (we're told old men are gay)
What has become of our astonishment.

The questioning of God's remote intent
Is still continued in the bloodless way
We wonder, now our early gift is spent.

O who among us ever would have dreamed
Our ideals and our bodies both betray?
What has become of our astonishment
We wonder, now our early gift is spent.

On the Seventh Anniversary of My Father's Death

The sun's light split the granite cloud
And rode with the numb cars and their ritual,
While I was hoping night would bring relief
To hide from me my insufficient grief.
I could not forget unfinished stories
He told among the pines and hectic leaves
That now, like light on broken glass,
Reflect those fragments of a fabled past.
Crowding the grave in the alien day,
Was it my anger that made me dumb
Or the way too many flowers were arranged,
Suggesting how death wants everything changed?
Although his suffering prepared him well,
And though it seemed that death was gentle
In removing mortal parts with surgeon fingers,
Was it his early joy that lingered
In that baffled girl with her whole childhood lost
Who learned his death in mother's shattered face?
She remembers his songs and the long nights freed
From fear by the spun threads of his fantasies.
And standing there in that insubstantial air,
Her wound bled in the veins of my heart,
For I needed remorse that would not yet come
To pay for the freedom that I had won.
The rabbi's words turned in my unholy ears
As light leaped in when the casket dropped,
And I stopped at evening's border, alone,
At my back the reaching shadow of his stone;
And my unproved love whirled about my head,
A dead father unsung, too young truly to sing
Or to see revealed where the shadows gather
The two of us, at last, at rest together.

The Parting Fire

Much time is gone, I speak of parting fire—
The swirl of sunset in the mist of trees.
Because you know affection not desire

Endures, you do not grieve when flames expire,
When night brings on our dirtied memories.
Much time is gone, I speak of parting fire.

An amateur of grief, not yet a liar,
My angered flesh gropes back to you to please.
Because you know affection not desire

Leaves space to breathe, you stiffen and attire
Yourself in contemplation to the knees.
Much time is gone, I speak of parting fire.

You say that spirit, descending, requires
Bodily gentleness for mortal peace.
Because you know affection not desire

Is tender in its touch, I too aspire
To honied tenderness—with stings of bees.
Much time is gone, I speak of parting fire
Because you know affection not desire.

Autumn Ode

This scene is the saved dream of the wind
That circled the drowsy boulders
As they swelled up in the sun, and chased the leaves,
Like children, to their beds. And it has rocked
The stiffening pines, and rocked the sea,
And blown the hour in the slow bear's ear
As he ambled to remembered sleep.

Like fingers of sight, this wind has stroked
The doe as she ate from the apple tree,
While everything below this noon is still
Or restless in the manner of its kind.
Goldfinches rise as leaves descend;
My mind alone is pained with thoughts of death,
Of dwindled summer limping to its end.

The day defies my gloom and so I name
Its changes with my eyes, and as it arcs
Above my head, it holds me steady
In its evening mind, another color,
Like the chilling stones, the leaves, the sea.
I must set thoughts of death aside, for with the wind,
This spent day is my heart's prosperity.

The Faithful Lover

I draw back when I feel the swell of spring;
The trees' buds shudder in their loveliness.
I sense a wilderness in everything.

Though not alone, I think of loneliness,
Of God's late isolation in the sky,
Lovers clutching each other's separateness.

So while we are together, you and I,
Abandon promises of future bliss,
And know me with the hurt now in your eye.

Regard the membrane-bursting leaf—a kiss;
Regard fidelity a passing thing.
It gives me courage when I tell you this.

You must not count on me for anything,
Because I love you as I love the spring.

The Frog Prince
A Speculation on Grimm's Fairy Tale

Imagine the princess' surprise!
Who would have thought a frog's cold frame
Could hold the sweet and gentle body
Of a prince? How can I name
The joy she must have felt to learn
His transformation was the wonder
Of her touch—that she too, in
Her way, had been transformed under
Those clean sheets? Such powers were
Like nothing she had ever read.
And in the morning when her mother
Came and saw them there in bed,
Heard how a frog became a prince;
What was it that her mother said?

Sestina in Sleep

There is a reason why the women weep.
The children play because they have to play.
The game remains, the children pass away,
And not the love, only the lover, dies.
Because this house has power to surprise,
It is not time, not time for you to sleep.

The game continues while the children sleep.
Only the lover learns of love's surprise.
The doors swing closed, inside the women weep.
The wind, outside, calls actors to the play;
Because the audience won't walk away,
It is the act, it is the act that dies.

There is new beauty in an act that dies.
Like dust in wind, each heart is flown away,
And one peers down the street with grave surprise,
Without the tears, and yet desire to weep.
The women ride like children in their sleep;
It is their time, their time has come to play.

The house, these chairs, are scenery for the play.
Brush back your hair, you stare with such surprise
As if you can't tell waking from your sleep.
Commotion of wind is never cause to weep.
Can you believe a dear thing really dies?
It is the dream, the dream will pass away.

If children, with their toys, all ran away
Because they could tell waking from their sleep,
Because they found their play was not a play,
That not the act, only the actor, dies—
Though not for this the audience will weep—
Then you would know, then you would know surprise.

Be still, the children do not feel surprise.
Their image gathers to another sleep,
Another act to keep secure their play,
For neither game nor toy, but child, dies.
The lovers touch; like dust, love blows away.
Now is the time, it is our time to weep.

Clutch your surprise, come tumbling into sleep;
Our waking dies, and dying goes its way:
It is love's play, it is for love we weep.

Love Song in a Child's Voice

O come to me sweetly
I've something for you
It has its own color
A red or a blue
It has its own motion
A rise or a fall
Though to anyone else
It is nothing at all.

So come to me gently
We've nothing to do
Nothing to speak of
That's false or that's true
Or painful to keep
A deed or a death
And to give it to you
Is as easy as breath.

The moon is a rider
That cloud is a steed
The night is their journey
The stars are their greed
For the night is with words
And comes in our time
Without any reason
And only with rhyme.

Then come to me swiftly
We've something to be
Not happy in length
But intensity
And secret as grass
And wide as a groan
And smooth as a snake
Unwrinkling a stone.

To the Family of a Friend on His Death

I have no words that can console.
Death is absolute, demanding no display,
No epitaph to shape our grief
Beyond the simple folding of our hands.
Love cannot justify our loss
And cannot keep tomorrow from today.
My friends, your sorrow is the stone
Of his finality. What can I say—
That he was kinder than most men?
That he endures in memory? A man
Is not the sum or fortune of his gifts;
You want his life. Somewhere some still break
Familiar bread in happiness,
Draw in the sweetness of abundant breath.
What good is it to know your early joy
Depended on his death?

Index of Titles

About the Author

Robert Pack has taught for sixteen years at Middlebury College,
where he is now Abernethy Professor of American Literature and director
of the Bread Loaf Writer's Conference. His publications include:

Poetry

The Irony of Joy
A Stranger's Privilege
Guarded by Women
Home from the Cemetery
Nothing but Light
Keeping Watch
Waking to My Name

Criticism

Wallace Stevens: An Approach to His Poetry and Thought

Children's Books

The Forgotten Secret
How to Catch a Crocodile
Then What Did You Do?

Translations

The Mozart Librettos (*with Marjorie Lelash*)

Anthologies

New Poets of England and America
    (*with Donald Hall and Louis Simpson*)
New Poets of England and America: Selection II
    (*with Donald Hall*)
Poems of Doubt and Belief
    (*with Tom Driver*)
Short Stories: Classic, Modern, Contemporary
    (*with Marcus Klein*)
Selected Letters of John Keats

Library of Congress Cataloging in Publication Data

Pack, Robert, 1929-
  Waking to my name.

  (Johns Hopkins, poetry and fiction)
  Includes index.
  I. Title.   II. Series.
PZ 3531.A17W34   811'.5'4   79-3651
ISBN 0-8018-2357-9
ISBN 0-8018-2358-7 pbk.